MW00334196

CANYON *of*
SHAME

The Bungalow Heaven Mystery Series

Faye Duncan

Jan-Carol
Publishing, Inc
"every story needs a book"

Canyon of Shame
The Bungalow Heaven Mystery Series
Faye Duncan

Published June 2022
Little Creek Books
Imprint of Jan-Carol Publishing, Inc.
Cover Design: Oxana Melis/oksdesign.com

ISBN: 978-1-954978-53-9
Library of Congress Control Number: 2022940968

Jan-Carol Publishing, Inc.
PO Box 701
Johnson City, TN 37605
publisher@jancarolpublishing.com
www.jancarolpublishing.com

To my late father, a lifelong mystery maven.
Sorry I couldn't get it finished on time.
I'll ask Saint Gabriel to bring you a copy.

Chapter One

It was early on a Sunday in September. The sky was as blue as hydrangeas. McGinnis, who kept his receding salt-and-pepper hair protected from the carcinogenic sunrays under a linen newsboy hat that matched his tweed blazer, steered his 1970s Ford Futura down the sleepy residential street of Michigan Avenue, heading toward Nell's Café. He and Nell had decided to spend the night separate since she had to get up at the crack of dawn. Still, he at least wanted to stop by before heading off to the racetracks. They were both busy people, and he had learned in his fifty-seven years that one way of making a relationship work was by simply showing up, even if that was all you did.

He pulled his old Futura to the curb and parked. He stepped out slowly, hoping nobody would notice how he was pulling himself up by using the frame of the door. The 310 pounds above his belt made such transitions increasingly difficult for the six-foot tall homicide detective. Huffing and puffing, he closed the rusty door carefully, making sure he didn't unhinge it. He walked to the café and pushed open the glass door.

Nell, who was behind the counter, looked up as soon as the door opened, and smiled. "Morning, Peter. How did your night go?" She dropped the dough she was kneading, came out from behind the counter, and gave him a peck on the cheek.

"Not as good as it would have with you by my side," he said.

As tough as he could be while working, he had a soft spot for ginger-haired Nell. He felt fortunate to have found her after all that he had been through with Lauren.

1

"What are you up to today?" Nell asked, running a hand through her untamed curls.

"Clocker's Corner. See if I can get a good tip for the races. Might as well risk a little bit, seeing that my career will most likely be over on Wednesday," McGinnis said sarcastically.

"Why?" Nell's forehead wrinkled.

McGinnis led her behind the counter so he could speak more quietly. "They asked me to testify. You know, the Tyrone Bastille case."

"You mean the one who is now paraplegic because your colleague broke his back in the Seven Eleven shop on Rosemead?"

"That one."

"Why would your career be over? You're doing the right thing!" Nell switched a button on the espresso machine and steamed some milk for a cappuccino. An angry frown replaced her usually bright expression.

"Just because I'm doing the right thing, doesn't mean I'll still be working there next month. Chief Bartholdo ordered the video to be destroyed. The only reason I agreed to testify is because Michael is my buddy. Otherwise, I would never do something that could harm another colleague. Michael's been with the Pasadena police for thirty-nine years. That's two years more than I've been there. He was in the patrol car with Fred when they took the call. Michael has the whole thing on camera and refused the chief's order to destroy it. That's why he's without a job now."

Nell served the cappuccino to a customer across the counter. "Last I checked, we live in a country ruled by law and order. If you do the right thing and don't break any laws, you will be fine," she said, then began filling a medium cup with dark coffee. She searched for a lid.

"That only applies if you don't work for a guy who has a history of violence himself. Everybody at the Pasadena police knows about the skeletons in Bartholdo's closet."

"No wonder he's trying to protect the guy who broke a black man's back!" Nell said, fiddling with the lid. She handed him the lid and the coffee. "Want some hot coffee? Take it before I spill it."

McGinnis took the cup. "Thank you, dear. You read me like a crime novel, don't you?"

She smiled. McGinnis put the coffee cup on the counter and carefully put the lid on.

Nell took another customer's order, then said to McGinnis quietly, "That leave any time to see you in between?"

"How about tonight?" McGinnis asked before taking a sip of the hot coffee.

Nell smiled from cheek to cheek. "That a date?"

"A date it is," McGinnis said, breaking into a smile that could cheer up a serial killer.

Nell almost sang as she addressed the next customer. McGinnis squeezed out from behind the counter and headed toward the door.

"By the way, nice outfit!" she yelled after him.

"See you later!" McGinnis turned around and left Nell's Café.

* * *

McGinnis passed through the open gates of Santa Anita Park. He felt at home in the old-fashioned, green Art Deco building of the twenties. *An epoch,* he nostalgically reminisced.

It was only seven thirty. The races would not start until eleven. He headed past the still-open gates and went through an arcade where, historically, racehorses had been stalled. The iron stalls were currently filled with show horses. Except for a stable boy who made sure no one stole them, there was no one there. McGinnis headed swiftly past the stalls and around the corner, moving past a few tractors and heading toward the tracks. He stood still for a moment to take in the view. His wish to buy a racehorse with his retirement money became more entrenched each time he came here. He did not need a house. Lauren was dead, and Nell already owned one. A racehorse was what would do the trick.

A handful of horse trainers were practice racing their horses in front of the backdrop of the San Gabriel Mountains. A few onlookers were scattered in the near-empty stands. Horse trainers and owners huddled together at the café and on the arena seats, analyzing the practice runs. McGinnis knew why he kept coming here.

"Morning, Detective. Working on any interesting cases?" Martin Seger, a co-owner of Snow, one of the star contenders in the stables, asked McGinnis after walking up beside him.

"None that I know of," McGinnis said.

"Just watchin', huh?" Martin asked. He was an old acquaintance of McGinnis's. They'd spent time together during the detective's many visits to the tracks.

"Yeah, maybe looking for which horses will do the best. You heard anything?"

"I'm keeping my eye on Behold. He is making amazing time in the practice races."

"Behold, you say?"

"Yes, sir." Seger nodded and walked away.

McGinnis grabbed a chair and sat down. He pulled a pen out of his pocket, opened the program, and made a big circle around the race Behold would be in. He could tell from the numbers that the horse was an outsider. McGinnis jotted down the word *win* beside the horse's name.

In front of him, the trainers were working out their horses on the tracks. Places like these made the detective forget that there was any evil in the world.

Then his telephone rang. "Damn it!" he cursed out loud.

He pulled the phone out of his side pocket. A few heads turned in his direction as he checked the number. Of course, it was the lieutenant.

"Does this have to happen on a race day?" he said through his teeth, trying not to attract any more negative attention.

"Detective!" he spat into the cell phone after answering the call. He listened, then answered, "Yes, I am well aware, thank you."

McGinnis stood up and shuffled away from the terrace in front of the tracks. He knew this was a conversation no one needed to hear.

"What? Eaton Canyon?"

"Yes," confirmed the voice on the other end.

"Where, exactly? I don't have to hike all the way up to the waterfall, do I?" Despite his size, he actually had nothing against hiking, so long as it wasn't for work.

"No. It's on the Eastside, right behind the Tennis Club at Kinneloa Mesa."

"Oh, shutterbusters. Right in front of the parking lot," said the detective. "It's going to be crazy trying to hide the body from the view of the crowd. It's a madhouse out there on Sundays."

"I've put some screens up," said the lieutenant.

"Great idea," said the detective. "What am I dealing with? Can you tell me anything?"

"A blonde in her forties. Shot in the head. Looks like she was dumped here. But forensics still have to confirm that. We'd need your input on that, too."

"All right. I'll see you there in a little while," McGinnis said, then hung up. He carefully shoved the race program and his pen into the pocket of his tweed jacket.

A dead woman in the canyon. Why would anybody put her where people would see her right away? Must have wanted them to, he thought as he headed back toward his car, almost forgetting about the lost day at the track. McGinnis had the uncommon ability of temporarily forgetting about his sorrows when he became absorbed in a case.

Chapter Two

McGinnis had just passed under the 210 freeway on South Baldwin when his engine gave out. It coughed, spat, continued on like that for two puffs or so, and then died two yards away from Foothill Boulevard. Luckily, McGinnis had the presence of mind to pull over to the side of the road.

"Goddamn it!" he cursed. *Quit the cursing already*, he then told himself. Even though he was not religious, he'd had the firm belief since childhood that bad things happened to people who cursed too frequently, especially on a Sunday.

The front of his car was hidden by black smoke. McGinnis held his breath and bent down in his seat so he could pull the latch that opened the hood. It was a tight fit for him between the steering wheel and the seat, but somehow he managed to get down far enough to get ahold of that latch. Then he sat back up, opened the door—which squeaked as if it were about to fall off—panted, and pulled himself up and out of the car. Gravity was stronger since he was parked uphill, and he hated it. He hated himself, too, for having given up on working out. He walked around to the front of the car, a handkerchief covering his nose, bent down, and opened the hood.

"Oh gosh—" He stopped himself before he could curse again.

A cloud of black smoke blew into his face. The engine hissed. McGinnis ducked away and stepped onto the sidewalk.

"I guess that's the end of my Futura," he said out loud.

He pulled his phone out of his breast pocket and dialed the Auto Club. "Get me a tow truck. Engine's dead. I'll need to be dropped off," he said when an agent answered.

"The truck will be there within thirty minutes," the agent said.

"That's great. Thank you."

"You will be contacted via text as soon as the truck is near," the agent said. "And please stay on the line for a brief survey."

Hell no! McGinnis thought. "Thank you. I'll just wait for the truck," he said, then quickly hung up the phone.

He nervously paced up and down the road. *I should probably call the lieutenant, let him know that I've been held up.* He dialed the number.

"Savalas?" he asked when the lieutenant picked up, just to make sure.

"Yes, that's me," the lieutenant said.

"I'm having a little issue with my car here. Looks like I have to have it towed. But I'm on my way."

"Where are you?" Savalas asked. "Maybe I can pick you up."

"I'm on Baldwin, just south of Sierra Madre. It should be really easy to find. There's no one else standing on the side of the road with a smoking engine. But no worries. I'll have the truck drop me off."

"Oh God!" Savalas said.

"Don't curse," McGinnis said. "I've already done enough of that today. It's bad luck."

"Sure, but I'll come and pick you up. We really need you at the scene."

McGinnis slid his phone back into the side pocket of his blazer, which, by some miracle, he kept wearing. The whole episode with the car had made him sweat rather intensely, and he now used his handkerchief to wipe beads of sweat from his forehead.

"Well, whaddya know," said the detective, impressed.

It had not even been ten minutes, and there came his truck. The truck pulled up in front of his dead car. The driver, a middle-aged guy who looked like he could handle anything hands-on, stepped out.

"You the guy who needs a tow?" the man shouted while simultaneously folding down the ramps.

"How did you guess that?" McGinnis said, then showed the man his membership card.

The tow truck driver took down his membership number. "All right then," he said. "Let's do this!"

Before McGinnis knew it, the driver was hauling the Futura on the ramps.

"Where to?" the driver asked when he was finished.

"Drop me off at the canyon. I'll walk from there."

"Eaton Canyon?"

The detective nodded.

"Sure. No problem. But what about the car? I restore old cars, you know."

"Seriously?"

"Yup. I've done about a dozen. Got a website and all. I'll fix it for you at a special price. Never know when you need the help of a cop."

"How did you know I'm a cop?" McGinnis asked, surprised.

"Are you kidding me? I live in Pasadena. Everybody knows it's the homicide guy when your car pulls up at a crime scene."

"What? How do you know about our crime scenes? I've never seen you before, at least not that I can remember."

They got into the truck, and the truck driver started it and began heading uphill.

"I'm a PI," the truck driver said, handing him a card.

McGinnis took it and studied the cheap logo, which showed a gun barrel and a blood splash.

"You're not supposed to notice me," the driver added. "I'm Zeke." He extended his right hand while he steered with the left.

"McGinnis. Peter McGinnis," the detective said as he stuffed the card into the pocket of his blazer. *Never know when you need an undercover guy*, he thought, shaking the man's hand. "But then again, you probably already know that."

"Of course I know. Detective Peter McGinnis, homicide division, city of Pasadena. I'm a big fan of yours." Zeke cleared his throat quickly.

A fan? McGinnis thought, baffled.

"So you want me to take a look at this car of yours and make you an offer for restoration, or what?"

McGinnis snickered. "What? You're a tow truck driver, a private investigator, and a mechanic all in one?"

"Exactly, man. I mean, Detective. You never know where the money comes from, if you know what I mean," Zeke explained. "I'm still just learning the PI business. I check out crime scenes when I hear something. More of a hobby of mine. My specialties are marriage betrayal and old cars."

McGinnis chuckled louder than the tow truck's engine. "Well, my marriage already went down the drain several years ago, so I don't have anything for you in that area."

"But maybe I can help you save your car," Zeke insisted.

"All right. I'll let you take a look. The way things are going, it's only going to land at the next junkyard, anyway."

"Great, man. Oh, sorry. Detective, I mean. I'll fix it up so beautifully that you'll wonder why you didn't ask me sooner."

What's the big deal, McGinnis thought. *If this guy tries to steal my car, he's only gonna save me the trouble of donating it to the next charity foundation.* "Okay, pal," he said. "I'll let you have it. Just don't try to pull any numbers with my plates and stuff, or else I'll have you locked up in no time."

"Don't worry, man. I'm a good guy," Zeke assured him.

* * *

Savalas, who had mistakenly been looking for the detective on the north end of Baldwin Avenue, had finally made it to South Baldwin. While passing by on the other side of the street, he'd seen McGinnis and the truck driver get in the truck. He'd honked his horn, but the detective hadn't heard him. He couldn't make a U-turn because there was a traffic island. *Damn it!* he had thought. *I'm going to have to head to the next intersection.* He'd accelerated and made an illegal U-turn before taking the freeway entrance.

Now, on South Baldwin, the truck stopped at a red light, waiting to turn left. Savalas smoothly pulled up next to the truck in the right lane, rolled down the window, and looked up. McGinnis looked down at him from the passenger seat in the truck.

"Everything all right, Detective?" Savalas grinned.

"Everything's just going great," the detective said. "I got a great man helping me out here." He pointed at the driver.

"So you don't need a ride, then?" the lieutenant asked.

"Nah, just wait for me at the site."

"Sure," Savalas said.

The traffic light changed. Savalas waited for the truck to turn left, followed, overtook it, and then sped off on Foothill Boulevard. *Strange dude, that detective,* he thought as he looked into the rearview mirror.

He had mixed feelings about McGinnis, who was technically his underling. He felt a little uncomfortable giving orders to someone who was seventeen years his senior and who had many more years of experience in crime investigation than he did. That was probably why he wound up doing all the paperwork, which McGinnis chronically neglected. Savalas felt that somebody had to do it and that it was more important for the detective to keep his mind free of such trivial things so that he could focus on the cases. The detective just seemed to have some investigative instincts that Savalas was still lacking. Because of that, he let McGinnis take the lead on many cases. Meanwhile, Savalas oversaw everything and made sure all proceedings were properly recorded, often without the detective's knowledge.

What amazed him, too, was the detective's private life. If it wasn't enough that his wife had cheated on him and divorced him, she then had to die in a car accident caused by her drunk lover. What puzzled Savalas was that McGinnis had never said a bad word about his deceased ex-wife. On the contrary, he had the feeling that if she had survived the accident, the detective would have taken her back with open arms. It was only after the whole episode was finally over, and after the boyfriend had been arrested for involuntary manslaughter, that McGinnis had begun to let go of her and start dating other women. And now, even when he seemed to be in a permanent relationship with the owner of the café, he still visited Lauren's grave regularly. Savalas believed that the detective's level of commitment was visible in his relationships, and he could not help looking at the detective with admiration. Because of that admiration, he was more willing to make exceptions when the detective broke protocol.

Savalas was pondering over such things as he headed along the mountains on New York Drive. Suddenly, he heard a horn honk behind his vehicle. He looked into the rearview mirror. It was the tow truck. McGinnis was waving at him from the passenger side. Astonishingly, they had somehow managed to catch up with him and were about to overtake him.

Oh my God, Savalas thought, *the detective is going to get there before me! I should maybe quit the daydreaming and focus on the road.* He accelerated. He did not want to embarrass himself by arriving after the detective.

When the truck pulled up at the stoplight on Eaton Canyon Drive, McGinnis carefully climbed out of the passenger seat, clumsily holding on to the door. Once he was on solid ground, McGinnis quickly waved at the driver with his hat, then marched down the sandy roadside toward the lieutenant.

Savalas rolled down the window. "Ready for your ride now?"

McGinnis, who had the choice of either being comfortable or sweating a little bit more, got into the car.

Chapter Three

"Oh, shutterbusters," the detective shouted. McGinnis avoided cursing as they parked right under an enclosed plant nursery. It was the only spot left. The small road behind the fire building and the Tennis Club was crowded with police cars, forensics vans, a firetruck, and dozens of people rushing around. McGinnis spotted the news van among the turmoil right away.

"Who called those?" he fumed.

"Must've been one of the hikers who saw the body before I got the screen up," Savalas said.

"Smart move on that screen, Savalas," the detective said. "Only a few moments too late."

"Well..." Savalas sighed and didn't say anything else.

"Oh shutterbusters. *He's* here, too?" McGinnis had just caught a glimpse of the chief of police, who was doing an on-air interview in front of a dirt mound and the black screen that had been put up by Savalas. *Fortunately, the body is out of sight,* he thought. *He's so dumb that he'd do an interview right in front of the body before it's even been investigated.*

McGinnis did not hesitate to intervene. After all, he was the homicide detective and was in charge here. "S'cuse me," he said to one of the news people. "Homicide. You need to back off. You are disrupting a crime investigation."

McGinnis glanced down the road and grabbed two officers. "Get these guys off the road. We need to close this off and record the tire tracks if they haven't already been destroyed because of these...idiots!"

To the utter dismay of the chief, who had just opened his mouth to say something that he'd most likely consider insightful, the two officers immediately prompted the media workers to step aside. The chief stood dumbfounded.

"Excuse me, Chief, but I need you to step aside. You're corrupting valuable evidence," McGinnis said, pointing at the tire tracks on the ground, one of which the chief was standing on.

"Oh," the chief said helplessly. "I didn't see—"

McGinnis simply grabbed him by the arm and pulled him aside, then showed the forensics team what he needed them to photograph. As soon as they were out of harm's way, the six-foot-three, slender chief, who'd always reminded McGinnis of a spider, pulled his arm out of the detective's grasp and brushed himself off as if McGinnis carried some form of germ.

"Watch it, McGinnis! I'm still your superior," Barthold Meane protested.

McGinnis wondered if the chief was so angry because he didn't get to be seen on TV.

"You are the chief, indeed, but at this site I am, sir." *Shove off*, he thought.

With that, McGinnis turned around and had one of the officers show him to the body, which was hanging helplessly in a dried-out bush on the other side of the dirt mound. She hung face-up in the brush, her long blond hair all tangled in the twigs, her face tilted crookedly toward the sky. Half of the body was balanced on top of the bush, while the other half dangled down from the branches. McGinnis wondered how she had wound up there. It did not seem natural.

"Must've got stuck in that bush when they tossed her over," one of the officers said to McGinnis.

"Clear case of dumping, isn't it?" Savalas said. He took two careful steps closer.

"It very much looks like it, but we can't draw any conclusions until we have fully investigated the situation," McGinnis said. "She could have been assaulted while going on her morning run."

"But the tire tracks?" Savalas said.

"Let's go and take a closer look," McGinnis said.

He climbed down the riverbed a few steps away so he wouldn't destroy the actual scene. He sweated profusely as he did so. McGinnis handed his blazer to a nearby officer and asked him to put it in Savalas's car. Then he rolled up his sleeves and climbed on, wiping his forehead with his handkerchief every so often. The edge of the riverbed had a bit of a slant, and because of the mound on top of it, the rocks and the dirt could easily topple down over the body, especially considering the detective's weight. To avoid such alteration of the scene, he walked around it, moved down into the dried-out riverbed, and then climbed a couple of steps up. The lieutenant literally followed in his footsteps.

When they finally stood in front of the body, McGinnis was panting. The girl's body was lying half on the riverbed edge, half on the bush. Her right knee hung on one of the branches, and her right arm slumped down. Her hair was entwined with the bush as if she had already become a part of nature. *They're going to have to take half of that bush down if they don't want to lose any of her hair,* McGinnis thought. Her head was tilted backward, her mouth hanging open as if to shout her last accusation at the sky. Except for a few scratches most likely obtained during her fall, there were no signs of physical violence on the girl, who was dressed in fitness gear and running shoes. The only thing disturbing her beautiful marble-colored features was a bullet hole in the middle of her forehead.

McGinnis took in the whole situation. Savalas stood beside him, observing silently.

"Whoever got her must have been a good shot. Not easy to get anyone between the eyes like that," McGinnis said after a pause. "She certainly wasn't running," he added, supporting Savalas's theory about the body being dumped.

Savalas asked, "So, do you think they killed her here and drove away afterward, or did they do it somewhere else and then bring her here?"

"I don't know. She doesn't look like she's been physically assaulted. Those scratches could have come from the fall. The medical examiners are going to be able to give us more info about that afterward. But the boys from the fire station would have heard something if a shot had been fired. Did you ask them?"

"They didn't hear anything. That's why I think she was dumped."

McGinnis sighed, but it sounded more like a harrumph. *This lieutenant is doing his homework.* He went on to scan the top of the mound. The surface seemed flattened out, as if somebody had put a sheet over it.

"You might be onto something, Savalas. See the top of that mound? Looks like somebody raked it or put a sheet over it or something. Do you see how the smooth surface ends at the edges?" He measured the distance with his eyes. "About the length of the girl's body. Get me a forensics guy to take some samples. See if we can find out what went on there that flattened it out. It does look like somebody came with a truck and unloaded their charge."

Savalas caught the attention of the forensics team and instructed them to take dirt samples from the mound. One sample from the flattened side and one from the rough edges.

McGinnis began crawling on his stomach up the hill. He asked, "By the way, Savalas, who first reported the body?" He was panting, holding his hat in his left hand.

"A boy from the horse stable across the street. On New York Drive. He was exercising one of the horses up here. He's not the one who called it in, though. It was his mother. She owns the stable." Savalas walked back up the mound and looked over McGinnis's shoulder.

"Oh, we're going to have a talk with them. They still here?" McGinnis said. He was breathing hard while lying on his belly under the hot sun.

"I don't know. But I have their contact info." Savalas seemingly couldn't stop himself from making a comment. "Excuse me, McGinnis, but why are you doing this? You know we have a whole truck full of forensics guys who can analyze the site for us."

No answer. McGinnis kept looking.

"You there!" McGinnis said to one of the forensics workers who was using probes. "May I borrow your tweezers? There's a thread of some sort that you guys need to take to the lab."

"Where?" the forensics worker said. "I'll grab it for you, Detective."

"Not necessary. Just give me the tweezers before I lose it." McGinnis reached out with his right hand.

The forensics guy, a baby-faced young man who looked like a recent college grad, handed McGinnis the tweezers and a baggie. "Okay, here. Take them."

McGinnis grabbed them, put his piece of evidence inside the baggie, and then handed it to the young forensics worker. "Thank you, pal! Take this to the lab and keep your eyes peeled for this type of fabric. Check and see if there's any beyond the edge of the mound or if it's any different there. Also, check on the girl's body. You know what I mean?"

"Got it, Detective!" the young man said.

"All right then, Savalas." McGinnis straightened himself up, dusted the dirt off his now-ruined Sunday clothes, and put his newsboy hat back on. "Let's go talk to those guys from the stable. I'm curious to hear the boy's story."

"All right. Do you want to walk or drive? It's right across the street," Savalas said.

"Let's walk. A little bit of exercise on a Sunday morning can't hurt."

The two investigators strode past the plant nursery and the fire station on Eaton Canyon Drive, then walked to the currently deserted New York Drive, where they crossed the road. They arrived at a sandy parking lot bordered by the iron fencing that enclosed the stable. The stable was built on a shallow hill right above the water reservoir. A horse trailer looked like it had been standing there for a quarter of a century. Next to it were a gray sedan and a white Toyota pickup truck. McGinnis stopped for a moment, took his phone out, and took a quick photo of the tires, then continued walking. Savalas didn't even notice.

They entered the premises through an unlocked gate that was hanging from its hinges. They passed an old, wooden barn structure on the right, followed by several open stalls. A boy of about sixteen was cleaning the stall of an old palomino gelding, which looked just as undernourished as the kid.

"Excuse me. We're from the Pasadena Police. We're looking for the person who reported the crime this morning," Savalas said.

The boy looked up, nodded toward the tack room with his chin, looked down again, and continued to shovel up the muck from the stall.

A fortyish blonde woman in a plaid shirt was standing inside the tack room oiling a saddle. She saw the cops but ignored them.

"Excuse me, ma'am," Savalas said. "We're from the Pasadena Police. We're looking for the person who reported the crime this morning." He looked at his iPhone. "Are you Fiona Sheridan?"

The lady, now out of options, dropped the saddle strap she had been working on, brushed her hands off on her dirty jeans, and reached out. "Yes, that's me. How can I help you?" she said bluntly.

McGinnis shook her hand. "We just wanted to go through the details with you. How you came to discover the body. If you knew her—"

"I did not know her at all," Fiona interrupted. "An' if you want to find out about the details, you're talking to the wrong person. Max there is the one who found her. I just dialed the phone because Max can't speak."

"Oh, I see," McGinnis said carefully. "Are you his mom?"

The tough-looking woman nodded.

"Are you also the owner here?"

She nodded.

"Would you be able to assist us in asking Max some questions?"

"Sure," she said, then waved to Max, who had been watching the situation from the corner of his horse's stall.

"The cops here want to know how you found that girl," Mrs. Sheridan explained.

Max raised his hand and slowly began to explain in sign-language. His mother translated for the policemen, explaining that he had been riding through the canyon with one of the horses.

"Max is one of the barn's exercise riders," Fiona explained. "He rides several horses each day starting at the crack of dawn. The girl was hanging on that bush when he rode up through the riverbed."

The boy pointed to the palomino, which was the horse in the stall he had been cleaning. "Buster," McGinnis heard the boy say. The name came out jumbled.

"He was riding Buster over there," Fiona said. "He's old, so Max usually takes him for short strolls through the canyon."

McGinnis and Savalas exchanged glances.

That sounds about right, McGinnis thought, then asked, "Did you know the girl?"

The boy looked at him with big eyes. Fiona glared at him intently, and then he shook his head.

"No?" McGinnis asked.

Max shook his head and then looked down.

"What about that pickup truck out there? Who drives it? You're too young to have a license yet, I gather," McGinnis said.

Max gaped at him in surprise and shrugged.

"That's Alfio's," Fiona jumped in. "Where is he, anyway?"

Max shrugged.

"Alfio helps clean the stalls here when Max is at school," Fiona said. "He's out on probation for a DUI and unintentional manslaughter. Had an accident. He lives, but his girlfriend dies. Poor fellow. Can you imagine? It's bad enough to get a DUI. But then your girlfriend dies because of you? I had pity on him an' hired him."

McGinnis broke out into a sweat. His ears started ringing, and he couldn't hear what else Fiona was telling him. He knew the name only too well. Alfio Cordini was his ex-wife's lover, and now there was another woman dead.

"We are actually quite familiar with Mr. Cordini. The woman who died in the car accident was my ex-wife," he managed to say.

Fiona gave him a disparaging glance. "Is there anything else I can help you with, Mr. Ginnis?"

McGinnis glanced at Savalas. *That was weird.*

"It's McGinnis. Any idea where we could find him?" he asked. He was desperately trying to keep his composure. He had had no idea that Alfio had been released and surely had not been expecting to hear his name in connection with any of his investigations.

"Well, he must still be around if his truck is here," said Fiona. "Maybe he went to check out the crime scene. I bet half of the neighborhood is over there."

Savalas and McGinnis huddled together for a moment.

"Did you notice anything before?" Savalas asked him.

McGinnis shook his head. "Didn't see him."

"Maybe he didn't want to be seen," Savalas said. "Let's head back over there and see if we can find him."

McGinnis agreed. He said to Max, "Just in case we can't get ahold of him right away, would you be able to tell us whether Alfio was here already when you arrived?"

The boy gazed back at him with big eyes, then quickly shook his head.

"So he wasn't here," McGinnis said.

Max nodded.

"At what time did you get here?"

Max held up his left hand, all of his fingers lined with dirt.

"Five AM?"

The boy nodded.

"At what time did you discover the body?"

The boy made another five with his right hand, then replaced it with his index finger, which he quickly dropped down to show a two.

McGinnis understood what he was saying. "Five thirty?" he asked.

The boy nodded.

"All right then," McGinnis said. "I think we got everything we need. Just in case we can't get ahold of Mr. Cordini, would you be able to provide us with his current contact information? We might have some additional questions to ask him."

Max and Fiona gazed at each other, and it looked like a game of ping-pong.

"Okay, I'll give you his cell," Fiona said, grabbing her cell phone. "Here." She showed Savalas her display, and he copied the number.

"Thank you, Mrs. Sheridan," Savalas said.

"Thank you, Max," McGinnis said.

"Go easy on him," Fiona pleaded. "He's only been out of jail for a couple of months. He doesn't have anything to do with that girl."

McGinnis and Savalas walked away.

"She sure is protective of Cordini," Savalas said as they exited through the gate.

"I second that," McGinnis said as he let the gate fall closed.

Chapter Four

While heading back across New York Drive, which was now way busier than before, McGinnis almost got hit by a black Mercedes that came speeding down the road. Luckily, the savvy lieutenant noticed the crazy driver, grabbed the detective by his upper arm, and pulled him back onto the sidewalk. The Mercedes was off and gone before McGinnis could see the license plate.

"Geez!" McGinnis snarled, nearly cussing again.

"That guy sure was in a hurry!" Savalas said.

They crossed the road and got back on Eaton Canyon Drive, heading toward the crime scene. McGinnis did not notice that the Mercedes stopped at the next traffic light and made a U-turn. He was too busy trying to figure out how the guy who killed his ex-wife had wound up involved in his case. He wondered whether things were spinning out of control, with the chief walking all over his evidence—literally!—and a personal acquaintance being implicated. *Is somebody trying to set me up?*

As he was mulling over what his old rival, Alfio Cordini, could have to do with the dead body, the black Mercedes approached McGinnis from behind, this time slower, almost creeping. Savalas nudged him in the side, but McGinnis did not understand the signal.

Savalas finally grabbed McGinnis by the arm and whispered, "The Mercedes. It's following us!"

McGinnis stopped and turned. Savalas put his hand on his weapon just in case. But to McGinnis's surprise, the driver of the Mercedes rolled down the window and addressed McGinnis in an overly friendly manner, saying, "I'm so sorry, mister. I have a bad habit of driving too fast. Are you all right?"

The driver had dark hair and spoke with an accent. *Something Middle Eastern,* McGinnis thought.

McGinnis was baffled by this unusual acceptance of responsibility, but he did not let it show. "You're lucky, mister, that I'm not from the traffic police. But you'd better slow it down, or next time I'll have them issue a ticket."

"Oh, thank you, thank you. That is so kind of you," the driver said as he turned the car off.

Why would he thank me? McGinnis wondered. "It's quite an unusual move you made there, Mr.....?"

"Farzem. Andrew. Dr. Farzem," the driver said as he released his seatbelt. "And you are?"

"McGinnis. Detective McGinnis. Pasadena Homicide Unit. Is there anything we can help you with? Otherwise, I need to ask you to leave. The public is not allowed here."

"Oh, really?" the doctor asked. He made no move to leave. "What happened?"

"I am sorry, Doctor, but obviously I am unable to tell you."

"Oh, that's too bad. I was hoping to find out whether the...the person you are investigating is my employee."

What! His employee? "Excuse me, sir, but I'm going to have to ask you to step out of your car and explain what you mean. How would you know that there has been a...that somebody got killed here today?"

Before McGinnis had finished his sentence, Farzem had opened the car door and stepped out. He looked way less relaxed now that McGinnis saw him face-to-face. Stressed out seemed like the better description. Savalas stayed right next to the detective, keeping his hand on his Sig Sauer.

"You're not going to need that with me, sir," Farzem said to him. "I am a peaceful man."

What the...? Who addresses a law enforcement officer like that? McGinnis wondered. *This guy has either dealt with the police before or is just unusually smart.*

"I'm an early riser. I heard on the news that they found a woman. Young, blonde, and from Sweden. Okay, the last part was my information. Helen was supposed to show up yesterday for a last-minute job, but she never came. Never answered the phone. That's not like her. When I heard the news this morning, I rushed over here immediately. Well, here I am."

McGinnis could not believe that the chief had let all of that information go out on air. *What an amateur.*

McGinnis said, "I'm sorry, Dr. Farzem, but I'm afraid we don't have the victim's identity yet."

"Can I see her?" It burst out of Farzem.

McGinnis and Savalas, who had relaxed a little bit, exchanged a glance. It was not every day that they found volunteers on site who were willing to identify a body.

McGinnis scratched his forehead. *Why not, actually? If he identifies her, that's one problem squared away.*

He pulled the lieutenant aside. "Go find Kimberley and tell her we have somebody willing to identify the body, will you? I'll press this one for some more information."

"Consider it done," Savalas said, then walked off to find the medical examiner.

McGinnis turned back to Farzem. "What makes you think it's her? Was she in some sort of trouble?"

Farzem hesitated. "Not that I know of. But her boyfriend worked around here. That's also why I thought it might be her."

"Who? You mean Alfio Cordini?" McGinnis asked directly.

Farzem nodded yes. "How did you know?"

"We're investigators," McGinnis said. "We're supposed to know things."

The comment made Farzem's forehead wrinkle, McGinnis noticed.

"Was he abusive to her in any way? Was he drinking?" McGinnis asked.

"Oh, not at all. The man was sober for all I know. Was out on probation for a DUI that went bad for him. Didn't touch a drop as far as I know."

"Was he physically abusive?" McGinnis repeated the question.

Farzem looked off in the distance, weighing his words. "Abusive? No. She just wasn't interested in him anymore."

Interesting, McGinnis thought. "Why's that?" he asked.

Farzem looked McGinnis straight in the eye. "I have no idea," he said. A strange smile danced on his lips, but it disappeared as soon as it appeared. McGinnis took notice.

Savalas came back, the medical examiner in tow. The tiny woman wore her long brown hair tucked under a hairnet, and she had on goggles and protective equipment.

"Somebody want to identify the body, Detective?"

"Yes, ma'am. This man here seems to have known the victim. Dr. Andrew Farzem."

She extended and then withdrew her hands, which were covered in latex gloves, in a gesture meant to greet the witness. "Kimberley Maddison, medical examiner."

"Dr. Andrew Farzem," he answered.

"All right. Follow me, Doctor." The medical examiner led Farzem toward the truck the victim had been placed in.

Farzem stared back at McGinnis as if looking for help. *Well, you asked for it*, McGinnis thought.

McGinnis followed them, Savalas in tow.

"I don't like all these coincidences," McGinnis whispered to the lieutenant.

"Well, this one was not that much of a coincidence. The chief basically screamed the case out loud on morning TV."

"You got a point there. But still..."

They watched Kimberley open the back door of the truck and hand Farzem a protective overcoat and a hairnet. "You are a doctor, the detective says?" she asked.

"Ah, no, not at all. I have a PhD in Social Sciences," Farzem explained while putting on the plastic overcoat. "But everybody calls me Dr. Farzem. My wife makes fun of me. Calls me that, too."

Kimberley frowned. "I see. Then let's do this quickly."

She opened the back door of the truck and helped Farzem in. McGinnis and Savalas waited outside.

"You sure you want to do this, Dr. Farzem?" McGinnis yelled into the truck.

"Positive. As a good employer, I feel that I have to."

A minute later, Farzem bolted out. "I'm sorry," he said, rushing behind the truck, where he emptied the contents of his stomach into the bushes.

Savalas and McGinnis exchanged a knowing glance.

"Do we have any water?" McGinnis asked him.

"Yes, I think so. Let me get something for him." Savalas walked off.

The medical examiner got out of the truck and closed the doors. She had a package of wipes ready. Farzem came out from behind the truck. Kimberley handed him a wipe, which he used to clean his face.

"Thank you," Farzem said.

"No worries." She sighed and waited.

Savalas came back with a bottle of water and Alka Seltzer. "Here. This should help."

Farzem took the water bottle and gulped down the pill.

McGinnis took a step closer. "So?"

Farzem looked at him, then nodded. "It's her."

His mouth contorted, and McGinnis worried that he would throw up again, but Farzem controlled himself.

"I am sorry about that," McGinnis said.

"What's her name?" Kimberley asked.

"Helen Johnson," Farzem said.

McGinnis interrupted. "No worries, Kimberley. We will send you and the coroner all the information. You can go ahead and close this scene up now."

"Sure," Kimberley said, then walked off.

"Why would anybody do such a thing?" Farzem asked. "She was inno-cent and hardworking. Very kind woman."

Farzem's facial expressions were distorted, so McGinnis made a motion to call Kimberley back for the wipes. Before he could call out, though, Farzem swept his hand through the air to decline.

"We are here to find that out," McGinnis said. "Please leave us your infor-mation so we can get in touch with you. Here is my card, as well. Don't hesitate to contact me should you think of anything that seems important." McGinnis and Farzem exchanged business cards. "And thank you for identifying the body."

"Of course," Farzem said.

"Are you going to be okay driving, or do you need somebody to escort you home?" Savalas asked him.

"No, I'm fine."

"Just remember to take it easy on the speeding. We don't want any more dead people," McGinnis teased.

But Farzem was not laughing.

* * *

While the detective had been taking care of his witness, Savalas had kept an eye out for Alfio Cordini. Even though Savalas had started working in Pasadena after Cordini had already been arrested, it had been almost impossible for him not to familiarize himself with the detective's backstory. Everyone at the Pasadena Police talked about it. How McGinnis's wife, Lauren, had run away with this Italian picture model and had then gotten killed in a car accident. And since cops had the bad habit of immediately checking somebody's background as soon as somebody talked about them, it had been impossible for Savalas not to see Cordini's photograph. Every cop at the Pasadena Police had Cordini's mugshot on their cell phone. Savalas had been shown that photograph a million times before he even got his first paycheck. The story was just too big not to have been gossiped about.

Savalas knew exactly who he needed to be looking for, but he did not see the man among the crowd of onlookers, which was thinning out.

"Have you seen him anywhere?" the detective, who was studying people's faces intently, asked Savalas.

Even though most onlookers had been sent away, there was always at least one person who somehow managed to mingle unnoticed, even with the professionals on site.

"There he is!" McGinnis almost shouted.

At that moment, a slender guy around five-foot-seven, who was wearing a hoodie, looked in their direction and then dashed away. Savalas immediately gave chase. Cordini headed past them on Eaton Canyon Drive, going directly toward New York Drive, which was now busier than before. Cordini ran across the street, barely making it past a car that slammed on its brakes.

Savalas was about to follow him across New York Drive, but the detective intervened.

"Let him run," McGinnis said calmly. He was holding Savalas by the forearm. "We'll get him later. If he was just released from prison, there's a case worker who has all his information and knows where he is."

"But he..." Savalas protested, trying to free himself from the detective's strong grip on his right upper arm.

"Trust me, Savalas. Alfio's not going anywhere. I'm not worried about him. Let's get back to the scene and deal with him later," McGinnis said. He released the lieutenant's arm.

Savalas could hear the pickup truck screech away in the distance as they headed back to the crime scene behind the Country Club, which was slowly beginning to clear up.

Chapter Five

Back at headquarters, McGinnis took a long sip of the hot coffee Savalas had picked up for him at a Seven Eleven on the way back to the police station. Savalas was leaning on the doorframe, arms crossed, carefully observing his co-worker. McGinnis was unconsciously chewing on his upper lip.

McGinnis finally interrupted the silence. "What are you staring at, anyway? Have a seat!"

"Do you think he had anything to do with the girl's death?" Savalas asked. He sat down on a wooden chair, looking as if he were attending an intricate math class.

"I don't know," McGinnis answered. "Personally, I hope he doesn't. Not like he hasn't been through enough already. But maybe he knows something, or why would he run?"

"But what are we going to do? The medical examiners won't have results for us until tomorrow morning."

"Work with what we have. Farzem gave us her name. I'm assuming he's not lying. So we can do a background check."

"Already done," Savalas said.

"Do we have an address?"

"1097 East Orange Grove," Savalas read off his phone.

"Bungalow Heaven," McGinnis said.

"I know. Bungalow Heaven again!" Savalas said.

McGinnis did not seem to notice the comment. "I say we check it out while we wait for the forensics info to come in. Do we have Alfio's address?"

"He's in Altadena. Next to the Rite Aid lot."

"And what about the Farzems?"

"They're in Sierra Madre. Little Santa Anita Canyon."

"I know that place. Pretty narrow. Never a place to park. I'm surprised the neighbors don't kill each other over parking spots."

"I know what you mean. It's best to leave the car at Mary's Market when you go up there."

"That's true," McGinnis answered. "That's why I never go there. Too much walking."

Savalas shook his head.

"Strange spot, though, for a foreigner to go and live," said McGinnis.

"I don't know. What do you mean?" Savalas asked, slightly irritated. He wasn't sure whether McGinnis was being racist or whether there was some train of thought he again could not follow.

"Well, somebody who didn't grow up here wouldn't necessarily choose the most inaccessible canyon to go live in unless someone brought them there, would they?"

"I guess that's true. Unless a real-estate agent managed to sell them a house there."

"Would you buy a house in a canyon that a firetruck can barely access and where bears visit each time you put your trash out?"

Savalas had to think for a while. "I don't know. Maybe if I'm a nature lover."

"Maybe," McGinnis said. "But a dude who drives a Mercedes Benz and nearly runs over pedestrians doesn't come across as a lover of nature to me."

"Maybe not," Savalas had to admit. He still wasn't convinced of McGinnis's argument, though. "Why, then?"

"Maybe the house belonged to his wife, and he followed her there," McGinnis offered.

Savalas still didn't follow. "Yes, but why does it matter?"

McGinnis looked him straight in the eye. "Resentments, relationships. Residences have a lot to do with them," he said knowingly, but Savalas still did not understand. McGinnis dropped the topic. "Anyway, where exactly in the canyon do they live?"

"They're on Woodland Drive, above Mary's Market," Savalas said.

"Makes sense," McGinnis said enigmatically.

Savalas ignored him.

"Who is his wife, anyway?" McGinnis asked. "If she has a house in Sierra Madre, she must make good money."

Savalas was a little surprised by McGinnis's habit of jumping to conclusions about people. "She's a judge in family court. Leslie Meyers."

"Who? Her?" McGinnis now stopped smiling.

Savalas was confused. "What? You know her, too?"

"She's the judge who divorced me and Lauren. Cuts up marriages like pork chops. If it hadn't been for her, Lauren and I would have worked things out, and she would have never gotten into the car with that...drunk!"

Savalas's amazement turned into bafflement. *Is he thinking what I'm thinking? Why is there another familiar person involved in this case?* "That makes two acquaintances of yours involved in this case now," he informed McGinnis with a warning glance.

If this was anything beyond coincidental, Savalas was going to have to take McGinnis off the case. The only problem was that they only had one homicide guy on the team in Pasadena.

"I admit, in twenty-five years of working Pasadena homicide, I have never had anything like this. And I have had people seeking revenge, for sure." McGinnis took his hat off and scratched his head. Then he took another sip of coffee.

Savalas's normally relaxed expression became tense. He did not like what he was hearing. Any personal connection to a potential suspect could put this case in jeopardy.

McGinnis appeared to know his thoughts. "You want to take me off the case because of that old story?" he asked.

What was Savalas going to do? McGinnis was Pasadena's best, and so far no case had gone unsolved by him. He was going to keep him on. There was no doubt about it. "Not on my watch. You're staying on. I'm sure there is an explanation for all of this."

McGinnis sighed in relief. "Good. Then let's get going. I want to check out the victim's house. See if we find anything."

"You want to get a warrant and do a proper forensics investigation?" Savalas asked.

"No. Let's keep it lowkey. Just you and me."

"Good. As soon as forensics shows up, the whole neighborhood knows something happened. Better go in there quietly. Let me grab the car keys from my office." Savalas stood up.

"Perfecto!" said McGinnis, putting his hat back on.

At that moment, McGinnis's cell phone rang. "Shoot! Who is that?" The detective checked his display and shrugged. "Detective!" he spat when he answered. "Oh, it's you!" His relief was evident on his face.

In the sticky air of the detective's office, Savalas observed the faint shadow of a smile dancing on McGinnis's lips.

"Yes, that's fine. I told you to do it." McGinnis stood up from his office chair and began shuffling back and forth in frustration. "No, that doesn't matter. What?"

Savalas shrugged helplessly, unable to do anything about the detective's poor phone manners.

"Sign a form?" McGinnis shouted. "All right, fine. Yes, I'll do it. I really don't have time for this right now. Send it over email, and I'll do it later."

Savalas left the office, got his keys, and came back with the keys jingling in his left hand. "What was that all about?" he asked.

McGinnis stared into the void. "What?" Then his face brightened up, and he smiled that barely noticeable smile again. "Oh, that was Zeke." He smiled from ear to ear.

"Who's Zeke—?" Savalas began to ask.

McGinnis interrupted him. "Come on. Let's get the heck going."

"Sure."

"You're driving," McGinnis commanded. He grabbed his hat, and off they went.

* * *

Half an hour later, the two cops arrived at the location, which was situated on the periphery of the renowned California Bungalow district. The building they were looking at was a more modern example of bungalow architecture, probably built in the mid-century yet still featuring that characteristic pitched roof. It was a duplex, with one apartment on the ground floor and the other on top.

Savalas pulled over to the curb in front of the house.

McGinnis took off his seatbelt. "You have any idea which unit?" he asked.

"Apartment B. The upper one," Savalas answered.

The two cops opened their car doors simultaneously, stepped out, and observed their surroundings carefully.

They were just approaching the house when McGinnis felt an itch on his right ankle, where he kept his privately owned back-up gun. To ease the discomfort, he pulled up his corduroys, loosened the holster by a hole, and then dropped the pant leg over it. Though he didn't see it, a curtain moved on the second floor at the same time.

Savalas, who was already standing at the steps leading up to the porch, turned around. "Everything all right?" he asked.

"Yes, just an itch." McGinnis had already broken out into a complete sweat from the effort of bending down, not to mention the heat that was hitting him from all sides. "Coming!" He stood up and quickly caught up with Savalas.

"Let's see if anyone is here," Savalas said, ringing the bell.

A buzzer released the lock on the door.

"Well, whaddya know," McGinnis said, thrilled at the prospect of somebody being there.

They entered a hallway and saw a staircase leading up to the apartment door on the second floor. They climbed up the stairs. Savalas released his gun from his holster just in case, and McGinnis knocked.

Though they had been buzzed in before, it seemed like the door was not opened for an eternity. The lieutenant and McGinnis exchanged a glance. *What's taking so long?*

Finally, the door opened a slit. The rectangular face of a woman peeked out. Her cheekbones were so narrow she almost fit through the slit of the door. Her eyebrows were sharp. Even though the woman seemed young, her tense expression and the shadows under her eyes betrayed her actual age.

Savalas cleared his throat. "Good morning, Miss..."

"Wawrinski. Marisella," the woman said in a grumpy tone.

"Pasadena PD. Does a Miss Helen Johnson live here?" asked Savalas.

Frozen like a wax figure, the lady on the other side of the threshold gazed at them open-mouthed, making the officers wait for an answer.

"Well, does she?" the detective helped.

Marisella thawed. "Ah, yes, of course. I'm sorry. Yes, Helen's my room-mate," she answered in confusion. "Why? Is something wrong?"

"May we step in?" McGinnis asked.

"Yes, of course."

The door closed, and the two officers were able to hear the chain on the door being removed. Then the door opened fully. Marisella's long, rectangular face matched her tall, slender build perfectly. A skin-tight, full-body black unitard covered her model-like figure. Only a black duster concealed the outline of her curves. Shoulder-length brown curls fell voluptuously over her sharp shoulders.

I wonder what Nell would look like in one of those...things. You don't see those on women too often these days, McGinnis thought as he studied the woman's wardrobe.

Savalas kept his hand on his weapon just in case.

"What happened?" the woman whispered, eyes downcast.

Both Savalas and McGinnis came back to reality.

"We are sorry to inform you that Miss Johnson has been involved in a tragic accident. We are currently investigating the circumstances," McGinnis began.

Marisella stared at him with what looked like disbelief. "You mean that she is...?" She couldn't say the words.

McGinnis stayed with her while Savalas began to look around.

McGinnis nodded. "Yes, I am afraid that Miss Johnson has died."

The disbelief turned to shock as she gazed straight at the detective's face. A tear began to roll down her slender cheek. "Oh my God! Helen... What happened? Was she...?" Again, words failed her.

"Well, like I said, we do not know the exact circumstances yet. We are investigating. That's why we are here. You don't mind if we have a look around your apartment?"

Again, Marisella stared at McGinnis. She wrapped a curl around her finger and looked around in apparent distress. "Ah, yes, I guess so. It's just... I'm sorry for the mess. We're both... I mean, we were both very busy and didn't always have time to clean up."

McGinnis looked around. "We are just trying to get a general idea."

"Of course. I am happy to help. Helen and I were very close," she said. Another tear dropped down her bony cheek. "I'm sorry. It's a little overwhelming right now."

McGinnis looked around. They were standing in a square hallway that led to all the other rooms.

"I'm sorry. I was actually just about to start to clean. That's why everything is all over the place," Marisella explained.

A mix of chairs, which had been painted by hand in different colors, were scattered across the living room. A wooden chest with a TV on top sat away from the wall. A coffee table and umbrella stand were strewn about randomly. The floor seemed clean to McGinnis.

McGinnis sniffed the air. The apartment smelled of incense, and there were two yoga mats, one rolled up in a corner and one rolled out on the floor. *The room feels very warm and full, yet something seems to be missing,* McGinnis thought as he studied the surroundings. But he couldn't pinpoint it.

"You practice yoga?" the lieutenant asked.

"Yes. We both did. That's how we met. At the Foothill Yoga Center. I'm currently working on my teacher training certificate."

"Those things are expensive, aren't they?" the lieutenant asked. "My girlfriend wants to do it, too, but she has to save up the money first."

"Ah, yes, terribly," Marisella answered. "It took me years to get the money for this. Finally, I am able to do it. With a little side gig, of course. I work as a receptionist at the studio, so they give me a discount."

"Ah, I see," Savalas said, standing near one of the rooms. "You don't mind...?" He was already in the room before Marisella could stop him, though.

McGinnis made a mental note to verify the information she had just given, then asked, "When did you move in here?"

"I think it was about half a year ago."

"You met her at yoga and moved in with her?" Savalas asked skeptically.

Marisella looked at him like he came from the moon. "Yes, why? Is there anything wrong with that? I needed a place to stay, and leasing a place alone was too expensive for her. This was the only way possible for both of us. We liked each other, and frankly I was getting tired of couch hopping. I'd done it for years."

"Nothing wrong with that," McGinnis replied. He always tried to look at the human side of the story. He knew that Savalas, who was very hard on himself, had the tendency to project his own values on suspects too often.

"Thank you," Marisella said. She gave Savalas a dirty look.

A cat meowed. It came out of the room on the left. The door was standing ajar. The black feline kept pressing its body against the walls of the hallway, its tail in the air and its back arched.

"Shadow!" Marisella went and picked the cat up, stroking it tenderly. "She misses Helen."

McGinnis said, "Excuse me, Miss Wawrinski. I don't want to be rude, but we do need to ask. Were you and Miss Johnson a couple?"

Marisella burst into laughter and set the cat down. "Yeah, that's what everybody asks. And I will be happy to tell you the truth. Even though I am bisexual, Helen was not. And no, me and Helen were never a couple. And never will be now." An angry wrinkle formed between her eyebrows.

"Whose room is that?" McGinnis followed the cat with his gaze as it entered a room.

"That's my room. You're not interested in that. Trust me. It's a mess. Helen's room is the one you're looking for." Marisella walked over and closed her door.

The door to the room next to hers was standing ajar. Savalas was still inside. "Now, that's interesting," he said.

"What?" McGinnis, who had crouched down in the hallway, asked. He had taken to stroking the cat, which had come back and snuggled up to his ankles. Now he lifted his heavy body out of the crouch, which took some effort.

The cat still stood there, and Marisella quickly bent down and picked her up. "Bad kitty," she scolded her. She scooped her up, dropped her in her room, and closed the door.

"This photo. You have to see this," Savalas said.

McGinnis went into Helen's room.

The lieutenant took a photo off of a pin board. "Look. Alfio Cordini."

McGinnis ripped the photo out of the lieutenant's hands, and Savalas gave him a warning look. He had almost torn the paper. He stared at the photo. Marisella, Helen, and Alfio were making goofy faces at a park, having a blast. Alfio had his arms wrapped around Helen in a protective pose.

"So it's true," McGinnis said out loud.

Marisella had apparently entered the room quietly. McGinnis gave her a startled look. She hadn't made a sound. *Sneaks like a cat,* he thought.

"That was at Farnsworth Park," she said. "We went there after we had the famous salted chocolate ice cream at Bulgarini's. Alfio works there." A minor frown flashed over her face, McGinnis noticed.

"I thought he works at the horse stable," McGinnis said.

"He only helps out there occasionally. His main job is at Bulgarini's. You can ask them," Marisella said. "She and Alfio were dating."

The lieutenant and McGinnis exchanged a meaningful glance.

Savalas asked, "When was this photo taken?"

"This summer," Marisella said. "Maybe two months ago. I might still have it on my phone. You want me to check?"

"No thanks," McGinnis said. "Not right now. But don't delete anything yet. I think we have a lot of facts to check, Lieutenant."

"Indeed, Detective. We do."

"Do you mind if we hold on to this photo?" the detective asked.

"Yes, of course. You can keep it. Like I said, I have them all on my phone."

"Well then, we're out of here. Please don't make any changes to Miss Johnson's room until you hear back from us, Miss Wawrinski."

"I don't think I'd be able to touch a thing, Detective," Marisella said sadly. "I can't believe she's...she's not..." Again, she couldn't say it.

Another wave of sadness seemed to come over her, and it fascinated the detective. He handed her a tissue.

"Thank you."

"Let us know if you remember anything that seems important," McGinnis said.

"Yes, sir, I will," Marisella sniffed.

"Oh, and just one last question. We have to do this. Routine, you know. Where were you last night?"

Marisella looked at him with gigantic eyes. "I was here. You don't think I...?"

"We don't draw any preliminary conclusions. We try to focus on facts, Miss Wawrinski. What I asked you is merely routine. I am required to ask all—"

"Suspects?" Marisella helped him out, a sour expression on her face.

"Trust me, Miss Wawrinski, at this point in our investigation, pretty much everybody is a suspect. And I do need to ask you this, as well: Where was Helen Johnson last night? Didn't she sleep here?"

"She stayed at Alfio's house," Marisella answered quickly. "Like I told you, they were dating."

"Well, thank you, then, Miss Wawrinski. And please, do remain available in case we have more questions."

"Of course," Marisella said.

When they left the room, Marisella opened the door to her own room to let the cat out, as it had begun to meow again.

"Goodbye now," McGinnis said.

Marisella walked them to the door. They heard the lock turn and the chain clink upon their departure.

* * *

"Are you thinking what I'm thinking?" the lieutenant asked McGinnis as they walked back to the lieutenant's car.

"Not sure what you mean," the detective said grumpily. He was growing increasingly uncomfortable with all of these familiar faces popping up in his new case. Plus, the heat was definitely not improving his mood.

"All the chaos in the hallway in the midst of a yoga session. And Helen's room is perfectly tidy. Weird, no?"

"Possible. I don't know. Maybe they just have very different personalities. I'd prefer to go by the facts rather than by impressions. I can't afford to draw any premature conclusions, especially now that I already seem to be acquainted with everybody who's involved in this case."

"That is strange, indeed," Savalas admitted.

"Coincidence, I guess." McGinnis brushed it off. "What we do need to do is check the information Marisella gave us. Maybe you could go to the yoga studio. And as much as I hate it, it looks like we're also going to have to talk to Cordini. I just don't think we're going to be able to fit that in today. It's getting late, and I would like to speak to Pepperstone before we talk to anyone else."

Jack Pepperstone was the chief coroner at the Los Angeles Forensics Department. McGinnis had known him for years and considered him one of his personal friends. The friendship between the two had helped resolve many a case, as McGinnis was able to get the information faster. The Helen Johnson case was a situation where he would need to take advantage of this valuable relationship.

The lieutenant gave the detective a questioning look, but then he seemed to remember McGinnis's friendship with Pepperstone.

"So, verify the info and be ready for Alfio tomorrow," the detective repeated.

"Consider it done," the lieutenant said, using his key fob to unlock the doors to his car so McGinnis could get in. They got in, and Savalas drove off. "Let me know where I should drop you off."

"At the flower shop," McGinnis replied.

Chapter Six

McGinnis flung his hat onto the Thonet coat rack Nell had picked up at a flea market, and plopped down onto the scruffy loveseat, which must have been at least twenty years old. *It still serves its purpose.* There was a bouquet of fresh garden flowers in a vase on a small table in front of the window. *She will love that.* It was about five o'clock in the evening, but Nell was not home yet. McGinnis stared into the unlit fireplace.

Alfio Cordini. Leslie Meyers. I know them both and like neither of them. And what was with that Wawrinski dame? I bet she's one of them hipster chicks, whatever they're supposed to be. She seems so sensitive and vulnerable. But what if she was faking it? Do all women start their yoga routine while cleaning? And what's with that mess in the corridor? Something is off, but I can't pinpoint it. Savalas is about the same age as Marisella, but he could not be more different. He is very dutiful and formal. A straightforward kind of guy. I'll have to ask him what he thinks, McGinnis thought to himself.

He was sitting deep in the loveseat when his cell phone rang. "Yes," he hissed into it after answering. He was too exhausted to spit.

When he heard the voice on the other end, he shouted, "Pepperstone!" He pushed himself up from the seat. "I was just about to call you!" He began to pace up and down the small living room.

"Well, it looks like I beat you to it this time," the coroner said.

"How did you know I wanted to talk to you? Aren't you off on Sundays?"

"I'm putting in some extra hours so I can take a longer vacation later on."

"Sounds like a good idea. Where are you guys going?" McGinnis asked.

"London, most likely. Always wanted to go visit that old house on 221b Baker Street, you know. Still looking into it, though. We haven't decided yet."

"Neat. You got anything on the body? How did you get to it so quickly?"

"I heard there was a body coming in from Pasadena, so I figured I had better take a look right away. I know you by now."

McGinnis gave a harrumph that came from the middle of his abdomen. "Cause of death by gunshot?"

"Yes, that's right."

"Do you think she was in any type of fight before she got shot? Any physical altercations, or are the scratches from the dumping?"

"No signs of physical altercations, no. Almost one hundred percent sure there was no rape, though I'll get that in detail in the final report. You're right about the scratches. They happened post-mortem. They wrapped her in an old blanket or something. The fibers were all over her body."

"That's what I thought," McGinnis said. "Anything else?"

"I do have something that will interest you," Pepperstone said.

McGinnis could not believe that after all these years his friend still took pleasure in beating around the bush. "Well, what is it?" he asked impatiently.

"Girl was pregnant, about six weeks. Still unnoticeable on the outside, but..."

McGinnis stood still. He was gazing into the fireplace, not noticing that somebody had arrived at the door. "Pregnant?" It shot out of him.

"Yes, pal. Girl was pregnant. Think that will help?"

Nell stepped into the hallway and just stood still for a moment, looking at McGinnis.

McGinnis nodded quickly at her to acknowledge her arrival, then said into the phone, "Yes, sure. I'm going to have to get some people's DNA, then. Awesome, Jack. Thank you! I gotta go now. Nell is here."

"Sure. No problem, pal. I'm on my way, also. Lydia apparently made roast beef for dinner. Bye."

McGinnis hung up and went into the kitchen, where Nell had gone. She was admiring the flowers. He gave her a warm embrace and a peck on the cheek. She blushed.

"Like them?" he asked.

"Love them. Especially since you're in the middle of a case."

"So you get it if I can't stay tonight?" he asked carefully.

Nell didn't answer. McGinnis noticed her slight frown, which she attempted to hide with a fake smile.

"I need some space. Things are different with this case, and I need to think stuff through."

"Are you in trouble? Anything I can help you with?" she asked.

"No, no. Just stuff I need to think about. I don't think I would make good company tonight."

Even though he could clearly see how disappointed she was, he knew that she would not insist on him staying. It was her ability to let things go that he appreciated so much about her.

"All right," she sighed. "I guess I'll be watching *Columbo* tonight."

He grinned a little. "I promise I'll make it up to you. When this case is through, you can have the real deal...all to yourself." He leaned over to kiss her tenderly. "No need to share me with millions of viewers."

Nell chuckled and grabbed his hips. "All right, Peter. Promise me you'll be safe."

McGinnis returned the loving gesture and kissed her on the forehead. "Don't worry. Nothing happens to this old house." He pointed at himself. "Any bullet that tries to make it past my vest will get stuck in here." Then he grabbed a roll of his own bellyfat, squeezed it, and released it.

Nell shook her head. A half smile danced on her lips, and she tried to hide it. He saw it, though.

"If you say so," she sighed.

"I do!" McGinnis insisted. He went back into the living room, Nell following behind him, and grabbed his newsboy hat off the coat rack. "Love you!"

"Call me!" Nell said before he went out the door.

"I will." He walked out the door, then realized he didn't have a car. "Oh. Can I borrow your car?"

Nell gazed at him in surprise. "Why? The old Futura finally die?" she asked.

"Motor died. But Zeke'll fix it."

"Who on earth is Zeke?" she asked, gazing in astonishment.

"Zeke is special," McGinnis said, not giving any further explanation. He started looking for Nell's keys.

"On the wall in the kitchen," she said as she hung her jacket on the old coat rack. It shook a little on unsteady legs.

McGinnis went into the kitchen, snatched the keys off the little nail, came back to the living room, and headed out.

"Be careful!" she shouted after him, all the while shaking her head.

"I will, I will! I'll be back before midnight," he said, then left.

McGinnis headed from the porch to the driveway, where Nell's 2002 Sentra was parked. It also wasn't the newest, but it would do.

He was thinking about how Zeke had seen his car at crime scenes, and he wondered which person in the Pasadena Police gave Zeke these tips. Then, suddenly, it occurred to him that during their phone call earlier, Zeke had asked him to sign a contract. So, instead of doing what he had planned, which was to go get a glass of Guinness so he could wind down and think, he drove back to headquarters.

* * *

When back at headquarters, McGinnis walked into his small office, where he closed the door and powered up his computer. He logged on, opened his emails, and printed the form Zeke had sent. He signed it, scanned, it, sent it back, and then dialed Zeke's number on his cell phone.

When Zeke answered, McGinnis said, "McGinnis. Just sent you the form back. Any progress?"

"Ah, the great detective! Your car is going to be amazing. Just found a new motor for you. From a racer. You will so love driving it. It will be like new!" Zeke said.

McGinnis was glad about the car, but it wasn't at the forefront of his mind at the moment. There was something else he wanted to get out of the way. "Listen, Zeke. I've been thinking about what you told me this morning in the truck. The only way you would know when I'm at a crime scene is if somebody from here tells you."

Zeke coughed and cleared his throat. "What do you mean?"

"You heard me. Who is your contact? Who tells you what's going on?"

"Oh, I can't tell you that. Imagine they'd lose their job."

"Not because of me," McGinnis said. "So?"

Silence.

"I'd just like to know. When I investigate crime scenes, that's supposed to be secret. Unless my boss blurts it all out on the city news, the idiot!"

"Yeah," Zeke said. "I saw it on KTLA. That was pretty amateur."

"Who?" McGinnis insisted.

"Not the chief." Zeke giggled. "I would never have anything to do with an amateur like that."

"Just tell me who it is," McGinnis almost begged him.

"Listen, Detective. I really can't give you that information. But I will promise you something."

"What?" McGinnis asked. He was getting annoyed.

"If you ever get in trouble, I will use the contact for you."

"I don't need any help!" McGinnis shouted. He looked around to make sure no one was listening.

"I know, Chief. Detective, I mean. To me, you're the chief. Anyway, I know you don't need help, but it can't hurt to have some backup, can it?"

It was rare for McGinnis to be at a loss for words. For reasons he couldn't explain, even to himself, he trusted this guy. He finally gave in. "Fine," he said. "Just focus on my car, please. I do need it soon."

"No worries, Chief. It will take me a few days, but when it's ready, it will be like new."

"Well, I gotta go now. Got some things to work through."

"Of course, Chief. You're the boss! Call me if you need anything!"

The only thing I really need is my car, McGinnis thought, but he felt he had already said that, so he just hung up.

McGinnis decided to call it a day. He powered down his computer, shut off the lights, locked his office, and left.

* * *

McGinnis was on his way to Lucky Baldwin's on Colorado Boulevard when he had a better idea. Tim Simmons, his favorite waiter, was not there these days. At least, he had not seen him for a while. *Must be in Australia,* McGinnis thought. So, instead, he was going to try the Delirium Café in Sierra Madre, which was a sister locations to Lucky Baldwin. From being an investigator for so many years, he knew that when you did not have any other clues, it sometimes helped to spend some time around the locals to see if any information slipped. Especially in Sierra Madre. In that little nest, chances were that somebody knew someone involved in the case.

It was already past eight in the evening, so it was an easy thing for him to find an empty parking spot at Kersting Court, the triangular town center that was usually full during the day. Sierra Madre was so family-oriented that most restaurants did not stay open past nine o'clock. But with Delirium Café, it was a little different. There was always at least one person who got thirsty past nine, and those people were usually not family guys.

McGinnis got out of the car and stretched his legs under the bell in Kersting Court. It felt good to be away from it all, even if it was only for a few moments. He knew that sooner or later he would catch the murderer of the girl. It was just a matter of time, and it was impossible to how many people would go down.

Finally, he shook his boots out and headed into the café. A few couples were still enjoying chicken wings on the veranda outside, but McGinnis preferred to be inside, where he could not as easily be seen. He headed straight to the bar.

"Bring me a Royal French 38, please," he said to the pink-haired lady behind the bar.

"You mean the stout?" she asked.

"Yup, that one. You have it?"

"Yes. Just give me a moment. I'll need to let it settle."

"Sure."

McGinnis had not noticed that a man on a barstool near him was trying to get his attention. Finally, the man tapped him on the shoulder. "Detective!" he said in an accent that sounded familiar.

McGinnis turned around, slightly annoyed by the fact that somebody had ruined his anonymity. It was Dr. Farzem. He was leaning over a pint of lager. Two empty glasses were sitting next to the full one. Clearly, the doctor had been here a while. Despite his frustration, McGinnis now gave himself a mental thumbs-up. He had sensed that he would run into someone here. He had not expected it to be Farzem, though. Maybe there was still some luck to be had in this forsaken case.

"Mr. Farzem, how are you doing? Are you all right?" he asked carefully.

"As good as possible when an employee was found dead in the bushes," Farzem said in his heavy accent.

McGinnis wondered whether drinking so much alcohol had made his accent stronger.

"The alcohol help," Farzem admitted, finishing the third glass. "Another one, please," he said to the waitress, who threw him a worried glance.

"Here's your stout," the waitress said to McGinnis, setting the drink on top of a coaster in front of his long nose.

"Thank you," he said, and stopped chewing his thin upper lip.

"Oh, let me take those away," the waitress said to Farzem.

"Are you sure you're all right?" McGinnis asked again.

Farzem did not answer this time. Instead, he just pointed at the empty glasses the waitress was clearing away. "What does it look like?" he eventually asked.

"Were you close to her?" McGinnis asked.

"She told me everything!" Farzem began. "I never asked her to tell me her life story. I only hired her to clean up my office."

"What was her job, exactly?"

"The official job description was office assistant, but she did a lot of cleaning for me and some accounting for my wife. In the beginning, my wife loved her."

"Your wife didn't like the girl?" McGinnis asked, taking a sip from his stout.

Farzem's fourth lager was already half empty. "In the beginning, she loved her, but then something changed," he slurred. "Why? Is this an interrogation?"

"Not at all. Just a casual conversation between friends of the lager," McGinnis said carefully.

"Yeah." There was an undeniable touch of sarcasm in Farzem's tone. "My wife loved her because she'd finally found someone to do her accounting who didn't charge a fortune." He took big gulp of his drink. "But then my wife suddenly decided that she was a threat, so she started to turn against her."

"A threat?" McGinnis asked. "Why?"

Farzem took a moment to think, taking a rather large sip of lager at the same time. "I don't know. Maybe she got jealous?"

"Did she have a reason to?" McGinnis asked.

"I didn't do anything!" Farzem protested.

Interesting, McGinnis thought. *He is on the defensive.* "Did you ever ask her why she didn't like her?"

"Just once. She accused Helen of snooping around. I strongly disagreed, and then we started to fight. Leslie and I never fight." Farzem took another rather large gulp. "She also said Helen was trying to steal me from her."

"Was she?" McGinnis asked again.

Farzem gave him the empty look of someone who has had too much alcohol, then changed the subject. "What was I supposed to do! She told me her whole life story," he whined. "It was getting annoying. I was trying to work in my office, and she wouldn't stop talking."

"What did she tell you?" McGinnis asked. He did not want Farzem to stop trusting him.

"Oh, a lot of things. She came here from Sweden. Worked as an au pair until the children were grown up. After that, she worked as an accountant. Then she lost her job. That's when she came to us. A friend referred her to us. Matt Gardener. He's a friend of my wife's. Oh, and she had this boyfriend. But I already told you about him when I saw you this morning."

"Alfio Cordini?" McGinnis asked.

Farzem glanced carefully at McGinnis, then nodded. "Yes, but I think they had broken up. She did. After she found out..." Farzem stopped in the middle of the sentence and finished his glass. "I think I better go." He pulled out a bunch of cash, which he plopped on the counter. "Before I totally lose control."

The waitress gave him a warning glance.

"You shouldn't drive like this," McGinnis said.

"Why? Are you going to give me a ticket?" Farzem snickered as the waitress counted the cash. "Keep the rest."

She looked at him with big eyes. "Thank you!" Farzem had left her a twenty.

"No!" McGinnis said. "I'm off duty."

"You are?" Farzem asked. "Then maybe you can give me a ride! I'm on foot. I live way up there in the canyon. You know, that cute place where the streets are too narrow for two cars to pass each other. Drives me nuts. My wife is crazy for wanting to live up there."

"So you don't like it in the canyon?" McGinnis asked. "Some people love it because it's close to nature."

Farzem shook his head. "Only crazy people live up there. That includes me."

Definitely has a sense of humor, this guy, McGinnis thought.

"Anyway, can you give me a ride?"

"Of course," McGinnis said before finishing his drink in one draw. He looked in his wallet for change, but Farzem made a gesture to put it away.

"Already taken care of," Farzem said.

Generous, McGinnis thought. "Thank you! Let's go, then," he said, grabbing his newsboy hat and showing the suspect out to Nell's car.

* * *

"What's this old car you are driving?" Farzem slurred disparagingly as he plopped into the passenger seat of Nell's 2002 Nissan Sentra. The cloth on the seats was looking rather worn. "Don't they pay you cops a decent salary?"

"Not mine. It's my girlfriend's," McGinnis said as he got in on the driver's side. "Mine is in repair right now."

Farzem looked the detective up and down. "Girlfriend?" he asked with a grin as they drove off.

"Yes," McGinnis said. "It's not what you're thinking."

"Why not?" Farzem asked.

"She's about ten years older than me," McGinnis said. "Stunningly beautiful and smart as a whip."

"Really? Yes, that's definitely not what I thought," Farzem admitted, then fell silent as they approached a seven-foot-high stone wall on Sturtevant Street. It led into a curve that took you to the canyon.

"Here we are. Little Santa Anita Canyon," Farzem slurred. "Or Canyon of Shame. Turn left on Woodland."

He had the detective's attention. "Why shame?" McGinnis asked.

"Old story," Farzem said with hesitation as McGinnis slowly drove up a narrow street. The houses were glued onto the steep hills like cardboard boxes.

Farzem said, "I like to walk to the town center on foot to grab a drink from time to time. Like tonight. Once, when I was walking back, this dude parked at Mary's Market and opened the trunk of his SUV. He almost got his hand stuck. He cussed out loud, thinking that nobody would hear him. Then he sees me approaching and suddenly changes the tone.

"He goes, 'Oh, I'm so sorry. I normally don't curse. I'm so sorry...'

"I thought, *Yes, of course you curse! You just don't do it in front of other people because you would be ashamed of it.*

"You see, that's the way the whole canyon up here functions. People have their homes, their pets, their children, their cars, their perfect little lives. They think that because nobody sees them up close, nobody knows what they are really doing. Just because people have homes and families doesn't make them good people. Everybody has a history; everybody has done something they are ashamed of. And they think that by maintaining their perfect driveways and perfect gardens, they can keep it a secret. But in this canyon, there are no secrets. The houses are too close to each other, and the narrowness of the mountain amplifies the sounds. People who live here involuntarily share their dirty little secrets with each other, and they keep quiet because they're afraid that if they talk, somebody will talk about them.

"You would be surprised by the things I have heard people say. The screwed-up arguments I have listened to. The many women who have been betrayed by their husbands and the many women who have betrayed their men. It is shameful, Detective. Elsewhere, you can maybe keep it a secret because the houses are farther apart. But in this canyon, you can hear people going to the bathroom. You hear everything. It is shameful. Anyway, ever since I ran into that man, I call this place the Canyon of Shame."

McGinnis was impressed by the fact that Farzem had not lost his train of thought despite a huge digression and five pints of lager. He understood intuitively that this man was intelligent and had earned the degree he was so proud of.

They had arrived in front of a larger two-story Craftsman a short distance above Mary's Market. He knew where Farzem lived but let the man show him where to go, giving him the impression that he was in charge.

"Here! That's my house. Yes, you can pull into the driveway to turn around. I know it's impossible for cars here. You have no idea how many times I have bumped and scratched mine. I should probably get one like your girlfriend. It would save me a lot of money." Once more, Farzem glanced around the interior of Nell's car in a disparaging way.

McGinnis turned the car around and then cut the motor. The night was so silent that he felt like he might be able to hear people breathe inside their houses. Some mystery birds sang their occasional mating songs.

"You hear what I mean? It's just too quiet up here. Not for somebody who grew up in Teheran," Farzem joked.

"I see what you're saying, Dr. Farzem," McGinnis finally said. "It sounds to me, too, like you should get some rest."

McGinnis had definitely heard enough. Even though he'd never asked Farzem directly whether he had had an affair with the Swedish girl, McGinnis felt that he knew plenty. He would have to come back for the paternity test, anyway, once this guy was sober.

"One last thing, Dr. Farzem," McGinnis said. "Since I am already here. Did you know that the girl was pregnant?" He asked the question in a very matter-of-fact way.

Farzem, who had already begun to get out of the car, turned around and said casually, "Pregnant? What? Helen? No!"

"Yes, sir. Miss Johnson was six weeks pregnant at the time of her death. Therefore—and please don't take it personally—I am going to have to ask you to submit to a paternity test once you're a little bit more sober."

Farzem shrugged it off. "But I'm not the father..." He realized his mistake instantly. "I couldn't be."

McGinnis gave himself a mental high-five. Spending all this time with the doctor had paid off. Farzem had walked right into his trap. He did know that she was pregnant—that was pretty clear—and he had lied about it. McGinnis didn't wonder why, as Farzem had even told him that. If the girl talked as much as he said she did, chances were that she had also told him who the father was.

"Do you happen to know who the father—?"

"I don't know anything," Farzem shot back.

McGinnis didn't really care, because he knew that as soon as they had the DNA, it would reveal everything. "No worries, Dr. Farzem. I am not accusing you of anything. It's a routine procedure, and you are going to have to submit to it no matter what. Someone from the Pasadena Police will be in touch with you about it tomorrow."

"Tomorrow?" Farzem scratched his head. It was clearly time for him to turn in. "Can't this wait a day?" he said, sounding uncomfortable.

"I am afraid not. The people will contact you tomorrow."

"All right, fine!" Farzem turned around and headed straight for the door.

McGinnis watched as Farzem clumsily unlocked the door and entered the house without a single stumble. *The man has self-control,* he noted. After he watched the doctor disappear behind the door, he turned on the motor and left the legendary canyon.

"Good night, Dr. Farzem," he said out loud as he drove down the curvy street.

He felt as if half the neighborhood knew that he'd been there, but McGinnis didn't care. Unlike the doctor, he had nothing to be ashamed of.

* * *

It was almost midnight by the time he got back to Nell's house. Her little white Craftsman stood quietly on the deserted street. McGinnis parked her car in the driveway and carefully closed the car door when he got out. He did his best version of tiptoeing when he let himself in through the front door.

"That you, Peter?" Nell asked in a sleepy voice.

"Yes, dear, I'll be right there."

He tiptoed into the meticulously clean kitchen, hung the car keys on the hook, and walked back into the entryway to finally remove his shoes. He sat down on the velvety purple ottoman that Nell had picked up at a flea market. He leaned back against the wall and stretched his tired legs out. He was just about to sigh in relief. *Wait a minute!*

McGinnis grabbed his right ankle. "What the...?" He quickly kicked off his shoes and unbolted the ankle holder. "Where is...?" he said out loud. He started breathing heavily, distressed. The Beretta was gone.

Nell, who was wearing a bathrobe, walked into the entryway. Her curly hair hung loose around her shoulders, and her gaze was sleepy. "What's the matter, Peter? Why are you not coming to bed?" She yawned.

McGinnis showed her his empty ankle strap. "My Berretta. It's gone!" he almost shouted.

Nell took the leather holster and looked at it intently, as if she could make the gun magically reappear just by staring at it. But she couldn't. "How is this possible? Did you use it?"

"No! I haven't used the thing in over a year!" He was speaking way louder than he had intended.

"Shh," Nell warned him. "The neighbors."

"Aw, screw the neighbors."

Nell's forehead wrinkled. "Come on now, Peter. Come to bed. Nothing you can do about it now."

McGinnis looked at her. Nell's fading beauty somehow calmed him down. He hung his tweed jacket on the coat rack and followed her into the bedroom.

Chapter Seven

McGinnis had barely entered his office on Monday morning when he was summoned by the chief. He had not exactly slept very well, knowing he had managed to lose his Berretta. There was no time to think about it now, though.

How did the old hypocrite get his hands on Savalas's report so quickly? McGinnis wondered as he headed to the chief's office. Discipline was not one of the chief's characteristics. McGinnis had never seen him up early to read any reports. In the past, he would typically wait to be briefed by someone so he could save face in front of the media. *But why else would he summon me? I wish Savalas didn't do his job so damn well,* he thought, letting another cuss word slip. *It's okay,* he told himself. *It's Monday.*

"How are you doing today?" Chief Bartholdo asked when McGinnis entered his office, welcoming him with a smile that McGinnis knew was fake.

"Fine, fine," the old detective lied. Nothing was ever fine when he had to deal with Bartholdo.

"I see a lot of old friends of yours popping up in your new case. I was wondering, do you have an explanation?"

So Bartholdo has read the file. Damn. Damn. So far, McGinnis had never had to worry about getting suspended. But that was exactly what this conversation was about.

"I'm not sure what you mean, Chief. I have nothing to do with anyone." McGinnis decided to pretend.

"Wait a minute. Let me see what it says here. Alfio Cordini, boyfriend of victim. How do you not have anything to do with Cordini? He's the one who was responsible for your wife's death!"

"Well, yes, but Cordini has served his time in jail. And since the trial at court, I haven't seen him. I have nothing to do with that man."

"That's what you say now. But when things get sticky, I'm the one who will have to stick up for you," the chief said.

No, you won't, McGinnis thought. *You won't stick up for anyone.*

But he said, "There is nothing sticky, Chief! We are following routine procedure."

"Well, I'm going to leave it at a gentle warning today, McGinnis. I don't see any problem with your handling as of right now. But if anything happens that is out of the norm, I've got Detective Orlando Lopez from the LA County Sheriff Department lined up. He's just waiting for my phone call."

"Fine," McGinnis spat. "Just stay out of it, and all will be fine."

"We'll see about staying out of it. I'm keeping my eyes on you. And don't drag that lieutenant of yours into anything. As far as I can tell, he's a clean-cut young guy. I wouldn't want a good cop ruined because his colleague is losing his touch."

"All will be fine, Chief. Just let me handle this, and we'll figure out what happened." For some inexplicable reason, McGinnis felt like he had never told a bigger lie in his life.

"Fine," Bartholdo said. "It wouldn't look good to the public if the Pasadena Homicide Unit had to ask for reinforcements in a small case like this. But if I notice that anything diverts from routine procedure, you're off the case. I am watching you, McGinnis."

"Fine, Chief. Can I go now? I got a case to solve."

"Go. But before you take off, bring in that lieutenant of yours. I want to have a word with him."

McGinnis had just been about to put his hat back on, but this threw him off. *What? Is he trying to set Savalas up against me now? What if this new case is not a coincidence at all and someone planned it to get rid of me?* McGinnis tried to calm his thoughts. *No, no, no. You are fantasizing. Nobody in their right mind would risk their career just because they don't like someone. Not even Bartholdo is that crazy.*

McGinnis raised an eyebrow and put his newsboy hat on. "Sure. Will tell him to come over."

With a sigh of relief, the detective stepped out of the chief's office. He wanted to go outside for a moment to get some fresh air, but he had to talk to Savalas first. Luckily, he was standing right there.

"Trouble with the chief?" the lieutenant asked.

McGinnis nodded. "Those old friends of mine on the suspect list are not making things easier for me. By the way, he wants to speak to you."

Savalas seemed a little surprised.

McGinnis helped him out. "He gave me a warning. If any connection is made between me and one of the suspects, I'm out and they are replacing me with Lopez from the LA County Sheriff's. I don't assume the same goes for you. I imagine he's going to keep you on board as the one with the hands-on insight."

"Orlando Lopez? Really? I know that guy. I worked with him before I came here. Guy's got a pretty solid record handling the drug dealers downtown."

McGinnis straightened his hat. "Oh, and I don't!" he protested.

"That's not what I meant..." The lieutenant seemed to search for words.

"It's okay. I get it. Our case is slightly different here. Not sure Orlando would be a good fit should they suspend me. By the way, stop by my office when you're done with Bartholdo. We need to discuss our next steps."

"Consider it done." The lieutenant excused himself and entered the chief's office.

* * *

While his new favorite lieutenant was in the chief's office, most likely enduring a wave of attempted manipulation, McGinnis took a quick break in the Spanish courtyard in front of the police building. It was the ideal spot for a quick walk, meditation, or just a breath of fresh air. With long strides, he paced quietly back and forth under the shady arcade.

Where did I manage to lose the Berretta? And if somebody took it, who? He tried to retrace yesterday's footsteps in his mind, but he couldn't remember a moment when he would have removed the gun from its holster. *Guns don't just walk out of their holster.* He could not figure it out, so he went back to the case. He stood still for a moment and gazed upon the water fountain. Then he took off his hat and scratched his scalp. He nibbled on his upper lip, as he always did when he was deep in thought.

The truck's tire prints! He tossed his hat back on his head, hurried back inside, and hiked up the stairway two steps at a time. By the time he was on the second floor, he was panting. He entered his office and called his old friend Pepperstone.

"Pepperstone," said the voice on the other end.

"Detective," McGinnis spat, as he always did. "You got anything on those tire prints yet?"

"Actually, you are calling at a good moment. Our lab just finished the analysis and concluded that because of the heavier imprints in the front, the tire must have been on a pickup truck or something that's lighter in the back. A tire analysis further revealed that it's most likely a Toyota or Nissan. Probably an older model. Late nineties, maybe. The newer trucks have larger tires."

"Excellent, Jack!" McGinnis shouted. He was mentally jumping with joy, which he expressed by swaying from side-to-side in his creaking office chair. "Let me know if you find out anything else about the victim."

"Sure, ole pal. We're working on that. Will let you know. Talk to you later."

After a brief moment of euphoria, McGinnis put the phone back on the hook. He grabbed the dossier that Savalas had produced. It was a printout of all the suspects, their jobs, their addresses, their family members, and, last but not least, the cars they drove. Savalas knew how frustrated McGinnis got with electronic files, so he'd had the wise foresight to print the entire thing out. To McGinnis, this was the most useful piece of paper he had seen in a long time.

McGinnis made a note in Alfio's dossier that read: *drives white Toyota pickup truck.* His feelings of joy quickly dissipated, though, for really, that was bad news for him. He had no desire to lock up the same person twice. And while his resentment of Cordini had been strong at one point, his common sense told him that Cordini had not been trying to harm him intentionally. Now the detective was altogether surprised to find the young Italian involved in another crime. *Something else must be going on here.*

Before he could think too much, there was a gentle knock at the door, and the lieutenant, who had been relieved from the chief's tirades, came in, ready to get to work. Anything was better than a personal conversation with Bartholdo Meane, McGinnis knew. Nobody at the police station was very fond of the chief, but as long as he was the head of the department, people had to cooperate. Even Savalas, who had a high rank.

"So, how did it go?" McGinnis pointed toward the wooden chair to invite Savalas to sit down.

Savalas continued to stand. "Bartholdo was trying to get me to report on the process behind your back, but I wanted nothing to do with it. I told the chief that we would add our daily updates to the online file I already created. If Bartholdo wants to know what is going on, all he has to do is log on. And whatever is not on there, he doesn't need to know. That's between us."

"Thank you, Savalas. I appreciate that. Have a seat," McGinnis instructed him.

The seat was a simple wooden chair. It was terribly uncomfortable, but the lieutenant reluctantly accepted the invitation to sit down.

"We need to find Cordini," McGinnis said. "Pepperstone says the tire prints we found at the crime scene came from a pickup truck. Alfio took off in it when we finally spotted him, remember?"

"Oh no," the lieutenant said.

"Do you want me to bring him here? According to the information we have, he lives only minutes from here. It's possible that he's even working at the ice cream parlor, the Italian *gelateria* in Altadena, right now."

"No. I am going with you. If anything goes wrong, I take the blame. I don't want you to be dragged into anything. And the entire case reeks of intrigue."

McGinnis was thinking of his Berretta. *Should I tell him?* he wondered.

Savalas seemed to be reading his mind. "Anything else I should know about?" he asked.

"No, no. I was just thinking." McGinnis slowly put on his hat.

"Okay, then what are we waiting for?" Savalas asked impatiently.

McGinnis took a deep breath and stood up. "All right. Let's go talk to Cordini."

Chapter Eight

Savalas drove up Lake Street, heading toward Altadena with McGinnis at his side. Even though the rising temperature indicated it was going to be a hot autumn day, the mountaintops were covered in a gray cloud that hung over them like a shadow. The cloud would eventually lift and give way to another perfectly sunny day, but like many other days in Los Angeles, the morning mist, mixed with the freeway smog, left them guessing.

McGinnis was staring out the passenger window, deep in thought, trying to figure out what had happened to his Berretta.

"Everything okay?" Savalas asked.

McGinnis didn't answer. He did not want to pull Savalas into anything. *Who knows. If this is a problem and he finds out about it, he could somehow be implicated. No, no. I won't say anything.* "Everything's as fine as it gets when your ex-wife's lover suddenly shows up in your case," he finally said sarcastically.

Savalas grimaced but didn't say anything.

Great, McGinnis thought. *It's working.*

After a steep ascent, Savalas finally made a left turn on Altadena Drive, which ran almost parallel to the smog-covered mountains. He slowed down in front of a still-deserted parking lot.

"Where should we go first? The ice cream parlor or Alfio's home? It seems he literally lives next door," Savalas said.

"Let's go to the ice cream parlor first. It's Monday morning, so he should be there."

"Alrighty," the lieutenant said.

There was no need to go looking for the place. The Italian *gelateria* was something of a cultural icon in Altadena, the little satellite town north of the city of Pasadena. Unlike Pasadena, Altadena was part of the Los Angeles jurisdiction, therefore outside of McGinnis's jurisdiction.

Once they parked the car in the vast paved lot outside the Rite Aid store, both officers headed to the ice cream parlor, which was located in one of the smaller shops. A brick apartment complex stood at the west end of the commercial lot. They peeked in the parlor's window but didn't see who they were looking for.

"Hmm," the lieutenant said. "Looks like Cordini's not there."

"Let's go in anyway," the detective decided. "Maybe the owner knows where he can be found."

Both officers stepped in, Savalas in his official uniform and McGinnis in a more casual outfit consisting of corduroy pants, a plaid shirt, and his newsboy hat.

"Good morrrning," the owner said in a heavy accent.

McGinnis tipped his hat. "Hello, Mr...."

"DiGiacomo," the owner said proudly. "How can I help you?"

"We are looking for an Alfio Cordini. According to our information, he works here."

"Yes, yes, that is exactly true. According to my information, he work here, too. And the man suppose open the shop this morning. I normally not come here on Monday. But the young fellow not show up. And if he show up, he get fired. Breaks my heart, to be honest. Fellow is on probation. But when you're in a tough spot like that, you can no afford no show up at work!"

"Is this the first time he has done anything like this?" the lieutenant asked.

"Yes, first time. But still, I'm business man. I rely on staff. How else am I going sell ice cream? Everything I have do myself!"

"I understand," the detective said. "But do you have any idea where he could be?"

"Maybe at home? I no know. He no pick up phone. Maybe you have more luck."

"His apartment is on Altadena Drive, right next to the lot here," the lieutenant said.

"Let's try there. If we get ahold of him, Mr. DiGiacomo, I will tell him you were looking for him." McGinnis straightened his hat.

"That I would appreciate," Mr. DiGiacomo said. "Everything you have do yourself. Nobody you can rely on."

McGinnis and Savalas exited the shop. Just as they headed across the lot to the brick apartment complex, an arsenal of ambulances and police cars, along with the LA County Homicide Bureau and the Altadena sheriff, arrived. Alfio's truck was parked on the street, the detective noticed.

"What on earth is going on here!" the lieutenant shouted.

"Looks like trouble." Before McGinnis could say anything else, the detective from the LA County Homicide Bureau, Orlando Lopez, headed in their direction.

Orlando Lopez was a short man with deep wrinkles, a half shaven beard, and breath that reeked of whiskey. *To compensate for the violence he has come across in his life, he uses liquor. Alcohol is the only thing that helps him cope with the things that he has seen,* McGinnis thought.

"What a surprise. Pasadena's very own. Good morning, McGinnis," said the LA County detective.

McGinnis knew this meant nothing good. "Good morning, Lopez," he said. He thought little of false exchanges of courtesy. He knew Lopez was not here on a vacation.

"And who's your partner?" Lopez looked Savalas up and down and wrinkled his forehead as if trying to remember where he had come across the familiar face.

Savalas introduced himself. "George Savalas. Lieutenant of the Pasadena PD," he said. "Pleasure to meet you again, Lopez."

Lopez gaped at Savalas. Once again, his forehead wrinkled.

The nimble lieutenant helped him out. "763 South Figueroa Street. The Gomez brothers. They assigned me to your case right after I graduated from the Academy."

"Now I remember. Thanks to you, we were finally able to bring their gang down in that warehouse on Figueroa Street. Not a good memory. We lost two good cops on that day, and I only survived because the bullet hit my vest and not my head. None of those cops ever had the persistence you did to keep following the gang's tracks. But where—?"

There was a commotion in the crowd. Somebody was screaming in Italian. "Alfio, Alfio, non è vero! Perché?" Several officers held the man back. He struggled against them but eventually complied.

"That's not Alfio, is it?" Savalas asked McGinnis.

McGinnis shook his head. "No, but he sure looks like him."

McGinnis and Lopez approached the apartment door where the commotion was taking place.

Lopez stepped forward. "Your Alfio, Detective, is here."

Lopez pointed to a man lying on the living room floor of the ground-floor apartment. The man was dead, bleeding from a bullet wound in his abdomen. A big puddle of blood leaked onto the cheap carpet. The scene was roped off.

"Let me take a look," the detective said.

McGinnis had to duck under the makeshift plastic barricade in front of the open door, grunting as he went. The three-hundred-pound heavyweight was not exactly subtle anymore. As he studied the fatal wound on the meager man who had once been his enemy, he felt confident in his theory that the several layers of protection around his abdomen would one day spare him from a fatal injury like the one the man below him had obtained, especially if the bullet did not hit him directly from the front. Alfio, on the other hand, looked like he had been hit directly—intimately—like a punch to the lower abdomen, only fatal.

Savalas came in and peeked over his shoulder. "Well, I guess that explains why the young man hasn't shown up at work all morning," he said.

"Any clues what this could be?" McGinnis asked Lopez, who then stepped forward.

"Somebody got him up close. That's all I can say," Lopez said.

Savalas approached the body and studied the scene carefully. "Wait a minute, Detective. Don't you carry a Beretta like that on your ankle?"

McGinnis did a double take. *My Beretta? Here? What?* "Yes, I do! Look, my Beretta's gone. I don't have it," he told the other detective self-consciously.

He lifted the right leg of his pants to show the empty holster. "I've been trying to figure out where I lost it all morning."

"Doesn't matter, McGinnis. You know what this means. I hate to tell you, but this makes you a suspect. Alfio was not exactly what I'd call a very close friend of yours. Everyone knows that. And secondly, you are operating outside of your territory, my friend. This is the city of Altadena, which, as you know well, stands under the jurisdiction of the LA County Sheriff Department. When the Altadena sheriff heard that there had been a fatal incident, he immediately called me."

McGinnis and Savalas looked at each other.

"My gun's been missing since yesterday," McGinnis said again, mostly just to confirm that it really wasn't there. He knew that Orlando Lopez didn't care what he said.

Savalas started at McGinnis. "What? You knew it was missing and said nothing? I thought we were a team!"

"I was going to tell you," McGinnis explained. "But then I thought it would be better for you if you did not know."

"Oh man, you should have told me!" Savalas said, looking the other way.

I have rarely seen him so angry, McGinnis thought.

"Do you have any proof of that? Any clue where you might have lost it?" Lopez asked him.

McGinnis went through the previous night in his mind. "After we finished at the scene, I went to Nell's to borrow her car—"

Lopez coughed. "What happened to yours? Your old boat finally die?" He nearly choked on his own joke.

Not now, McGinnis thought. "It's in repair," he simply said, then went on. "Then I drove to the office to print something." He prayed that Lopez wouldn't ask what, and the alcoholic detective didn't bother. "Then I drove to the Delirium Café in Sierra Madre."

"Why the Delirium?" Lopez asked. "Don't you usually hang out at Lucky Baldwin's on Colorado?"

"Yes, that's true. But I thought I'd change up the old routine. My buddy at the one on Colorado isn't there these days." McGinnis hoped that made his choice sound more credible. He knew well enough not to mention his conversation with Farzem that night. He was not going to throw away that amazing source of information by giving it all away to Lopez.

Luckily, they did not call McGinnis's bluff. Savalas was as silent as a mouse.

"And then what?" Lopez asked. He seemed to be at an utter loss over what to do about his colleague's dilemma.

"I went back to Nell's."

"So when *did* you realize you didn't have a gun? Or did Nell have to explain that to you, too?"

McGinnis did not appreciate what he was implying. "No," he said. "I noticed that it was missing when I got undressed. You can call her if you want. She'll tell you. I still can't believe I didn't notice before."

"Well, I'm going to have to take you to my downtown office to record your testimony." Then he shouted out to one of his colleages, Sergeant!"

"Yes, sir?" the cop responded.

"I'm taking this one here to HQ. You take care of everything else here and report to me as soon as you get there, okay?"

"Sure, boss," the sergeant said.

"Wait a minute," Savalas interjected before Lopez escorted the detective away. "I need a word with him."

Lopez turned and stared at the lieutenant as if he had asked him to quit drinking alcohol, but he complied. There was no question that Savalas's request was perfectly sound.

"What do you want me to do?" Savalas asked McGinnis quietly.

McGinnis whispered, "Get information from the guy who looks like Alfio. We'll need to talk to him."

"Already done," Savalas whispered back.

Lopez quickly shoved McGinnis into the back of his squad car.

McGinnis almost scraped his head on the doorframe, but somehow he managed to grab his hat before it fell to the ground. "Sorry, I can't lose this. Nell gave it to me. It's sentimental."

Lopez shook his head, grabbed his flask from the inside of his chest pocket, and took a swig. "Want some?"

McGinnis declined.

* * *

"So what's her telephone number?" Lopez asked McGinnis about forty-five minutes later, after they had arrived downtown and were in his office at the LASD headquarters on Temple Street.

"Whose number?" McGinnis asked. The two homicide detectives hadn't talked about anything related to the case during the ride, so Lopez's question now surprised him.

"Nell's, man! Who else's? I'm going to call her to get a testimony, and then I'm going to send you back home with the first officer available. I don't have time to waste on your petty relationships. If Bartholdo wants to suspend you, let him. But quite frankly, if he wants your case solved, he shouldn't. You're the only one who is going to do it."

With a sigh of relief, McGinnis grabbed a pencil and paper from Lopez's desk and scribbled a phone number on it. "Try her at the café. She won't be home now, and her cell phone's probably off."

Lopez dialed the number. "Yes, this is Detective Lopez from the Los Angeles Sheriff Department. I would like to speak to a Nell..." He covered the speaker. "What's her full name?"

Before McGinnis was able to answer, a loud voice said, "Speaking! What...? Is this about Peter?"

McGinnis heard the concern in Nell's voice. Embarrassed, he began chewing his upper lip.

Lopez did not waste any time. "Yes, Miss Nell, it's about McGinnis. And I'm really sorry to bother you. But did you notice anything about your... about McGinnis last night that was unusual or out of the ordinary?"

"Out of the ordinary?" Nell repeated. "He didn't have his gun!" It shot out of her. "He thought he might have misplaced it somewhere, but if you ask me, somebody stole it at the bar. He never touches that thing except in the morning when he gets dressed and at night when he undresses. Why are you asking? Is he in some sort of trouble or something?"

"No, actually. You might have just saved him from getting arrested. At least, as far as I am concerned."

"Arrested?" she shouted. "Can I speak with him for a moment?"

Lopez handed the phone to McGinnis.

"What's the matter, Peter? What's this talk about you getting arrested?"

"Oh, I think you may have just saved me from it. Though I'm not one hundred percent sure yet. Somebody planted my gun next to Alfio's body."

"You mean Alfio Cordini is also dead?"

"Yes, I'm afraid that is so."

"I'm worried about you, Peter. Things have never been so personal."

Lopez took a swig from his flask and offered some to McGinnis. McGinnis gently declined.

"I know, dear. But all will be well. Detective Lopez here is taking great care of me," he said.

The sarcasm in McGinnis's tone prompted Lopez to abruptly ask for the phone back.

"I gotta go now. Yes, I will see you later."

"Thank you so much for helping us out here, Miss Nell," Lopez said when he took the phone back. "You should have your detective back right on time for dinner." He dumped the phone onto its charging station, then turned to McGinnis. "All right, McGinnis, give me her full name, and you're off the hook. I don't have time for this nonsense."

McGinnis scribbled Nell's name on the paper where he'd written her number.

Lopez glanced at the paper and said, "Great! I'll have Ramirez drive you back to Pasadena. I'll see if we can find the thief of that gun of yours."

"Murderer," McGinnis corrected him.

"Exactly," said Lopez. "So our cases are connected, you say?"

"They were dating," McGinnis explained to him. "Savalas has a photo. There's a roommate and the girl's employers, and she was six weeks pregnant. I will have Savalas send you the file as soon as I get back."

"Boyfriend and girlfriend dead, but not at the same time? That's strange."

"Definitely not a murder-suicide, if that's what you're thinking," McGinnis said.

"You think it's a suicide?" Lopez asked.

"Now that Alfio is also dead, it could be. He could have killed her first and then himself after he saw the consequences coming. But I doubt it.

Definitely don't see how he would have gotten that gun of mine." McGinnis took off his newsboy hat and scratched his head. The disappearance of his gun truly flustered him.

"Anyway," said Lopez. "I'll help you catch the thief of that gun of yours and take a look at what you have so far, but I bet that once we have the thief, the case will be back on your desk."

Officer Ramirez appeared at the door. "You called?" he said.

"This is Detective McGinnis from Pasadena. Drive him back home," Lopez ordered. "He's done here."

"Heard a lot about you. Great to meet you, Detective." Ramirez extended his hand.

McGinnis gave his hand a good shake. "Thanks, Officer. Your generation is the future of law enforcement, not old houses like me."

The young officer stood there, somewhat dumbstruck by McGinnis's wise words.

"Okay, let's go now!" Lopez helped them out, drawing a flask of whiskey from his chest pocket.

McGinnis and Ramirez both pretended like they did not see.

Chapter Nine

McGinnis was back in his office in Pasadena early the next day. The stolen gun had him more worried than not. After so many years of masterfully maneuvering through countless cases, he felt like he finally may have lost sight of the bigger picture. *Maybe Bartholdo is right. I have lost my touch.*

What he knew was that he needed to talk to the man who'd been in front of Alfio's apartment. He grabbed the Savalas dossier and looked up Cordini. Sure enough, Mauro Cordini, thirty-two years old, was listed. *His brother.* Alfio had been two years his senior. *What a tragedy. No one deserves that, not even your worst enemy,* he thought to himself ironically.

McGinnis looked up. "Well, good afternoon, Savalas." The handsome cop was standing in the detective's doorframe.

"They let you go?" Savalas asked.

"I have an alibi," McGinnis said.

"Nell?" Savalas asked.

McGinnis nodded.

"You're a *lucky* man," Savalas said.

Still, the trouble was not out of the way just yet. McGinnis was still looking forward to his face-off with Bartholdo.

"Did you ever get ahold of Alfio's brother? We need to talk to him," McGinnis said.

"Actually, I did. He's staying at the neighbor's house while they clean up the scene."

"Let's go talk to him. I wonder what he knows."

Savalas pulled his keys from his pocket and dangled them over McGinnis's head. "Still no car?"

"No," McGinnis said grumpily. "Let's go."

* * *

The two cops headed once more to Lake Street and parked in the same lot that had caused so much turmoil the previous day. It was all quiet now. They stepped out and approached the apartment building. McGinnis lingered somewhat indecisively in front of the apartment, where a bio-cleanup truck was parked.

"Over here!" Savalas said.

McGinnis jerked his head as if he had been awoken from a daydream. "Sure."

Savalas rang the bell. They could hear the shuffling of steps moving toward the door. Savalas kept his hand on his holster just to be safe. The door opened a crack. McGinnis recognized the face instantly.

"Mr. Cordini?" Savalas said.

"I already told you everything. What do you want?"

"We would just like to ask you a few more questions about your brother. By the way, I am very sorry for your loss," McGinnis said.

Mauro looked at McGinnis with big eyes, then covered his eyes with his hand and shook his head. He opened the door. "All right. Come on in. Make it quick. This is not my place. There's a baby sleeping in another room."

McGinnis watched a man and a woman peek in through the kitchen door.

"Can we close that?" Savalas said.

Mauro went and closed the door.

"Thank you, Mr. Cordini," McGinnis said.

"And thank you for taking the time to talk to us. I understand how upsetting this must be to you. Are we assuming correctly that you learned of your brother's death at the moment we were present at the scene?" Savalas said.

Mauro nodded his head. They were all standing uncomfortably in a poorly furnished living room.

"Antonella call me. I work. She say she hear a shot. She also call the sheriff."

Savalas nodded to McGinnis, who thought, *Yes, it was Antonella who had called the Altadena Sheriff Station.*

Mauro went on, "I immediately come to see if it is Alfio. He no deserve to die. Not after he just get out. It is all Helen's fault."

"Why is it her fault?" McGinnis asked.

"That girl is trouble. She sleep with every man she see. First, her first boss, the doctor from Pasadena. Then the guy from Sierra Madre. Why Alfio have to die, I no know." Mauro sighed.

"Who was her first boss?" Savalas asked.

"Matt Gardener, a physician. He pay her for years, but no work."

McGinnis looked at Savalas. "We're going to have to talk to him."

Savalas nodded.

"Are you aware that Helen Johnson has been murdered?"

Mauro gazed at McGinnis in shock. "What? Helen is also dead? Madre mia, no!" He looked at McGinnis, then at Savalas, then started to bawl. "Alfio was mia only famiglia. Perché?" Mauro sat down on the armrest of a worn-out armchair.

McGinnis glanced at Savalas. *That's enough for today.* "All right, Mr. Cordini. We would just need to have a word with Miss Antonella."

The door to the kitchen opened quietly. "Mossi. I am Antonella Mossi. I call the sheriff."

"Thank you for reporting it immediately. At what time did you hear the shot?" McGinnis said.

"It was in the morning. Maybe nine o'clock. It was not loud. Almost like something fall on the floor."

"In the middle of a business day?" Savalas asked.

"Yes, that's odd. Why would anybody risk getting caught in bright daylight," McGinnis said.

"Well, it definitely clears you since you were on the way to the ice cream shop with me when it happened," Savalas said.

"Had we arrived only a few minutes earlier, we could have saved his life!" McGinnis sighed.

"I call immediately when I hear it," Antonella Mossi repeated.

"Did you hear anything else that was suspicious?"

"Yes, there was noise in the kitchen, like glass break or something."

"Is your apartment the same as Mr. Cordini's?" McGinnis asked.

Mrs. Mossi nodded. "Same, yes."

"You don't mind if we have a look, do you?"

"My husband is in kitchen. Wait a moment. Claudio?"

McGinnis heard the scratching of a chair leg against the kitchen floor.

"Si, I'm coming." A heavyset man dressed in his underwear came into the room. A baby began to cry.

"Detective, look at kitchen," Claudio Mossi said. "Me go and look after Toto." The man left the living room.

McGinnis studied the kitchen window. It was a simple sliding window covered by a screen on the outside. The window was just above a double sink. "Perfect escape if you don't want to be seen," he said. "Where does it lead to?"

They looked outside. A narrow pathway separated the apartment complex from a wooded hill beyond.

"Let's go and check the window screen. We'll have to talk more about that with Lopez," McGinnis said, then left the kitchen. Savalas followed him. "Thank you so much, Mrs. Mossi. You have helped a lot. If you remember any details, don't hesitate to call me or Detective Lopez." He handed her his card.

Mauro was sitting in the old armchair with his head buried in his hands.

"Goodbye, Mr. Cordini. We are very sorry," McGinnis said.

Mauro briefly looked up. His face was puffy from grief and tears.

McGinnis and Savalas left the apartment.

"So how do we get behind there?" McGinnis asked.

"You go left, and I go right."

The two cops split up, and a minute later Savalas shouted, "I think I found it."

McGinnis came around the other corner and met Savalas at the kitchen window. The window screen was on the ground.

"I think we should let Lopez know that we have a piece of evidence," Savalas said.

They took pictures of the screen and the window.

"Look, footprints!" Savalas pointed to the soft ground above the retaining wall.

"Take some pictures," McGinnis said. "Small man or larger woman, I would say. Not sure if you can say what kind of footwear. Would have to ask forensics to take a look."

"I wonder if Lopez caught all this," Savalas said.

Savalas jumped onto the retaining wall and followed the steps up the hill. He went several yards into a wooded area full of pines. McGinnis stayed in place. No way could he get onto that wall without help.

"I lose them here. Too many pines." Savalas took some more pictures, most likely to note how far into the forest he was able to follow the prints.

"All right, let's head back," McGinnis said.

As they headed to Savalas's car, McGinnis pulled out his phone and called Lopez. "Orlando, it's McGinnis from the Pasadena PD. We have some questions," he said, this time without spitting, when Lopez answered.

Savalas and McGinnis reached the car. Savalas unlocked it, and McGinnis got into the passenger seat, attempting to hold his breath. He did not want to pant into the telephone line. He briefly covered up the speaker and exhaled noticeably. He then put the phone back to his ear.

"Did you check in the kitchen? We are thinking the shooter most likely escaped through the kitchen window. We found the screen on the ground. And there are footprints in the woods," McGinnis said.

"Footprints? Didn't occur to us to look on the outside. Yes, there were broken plants and dishes all around the sink and the sill. The killer clearly escaped through that window. I'll send forensics over to take the footprints."

"Not necessary. We have the photos."

"Perfect. Then send them over, will you?"

Savalas started the engine, and McGinnis glanced at him and said, "Savalas will do that as soon as he gets to his desk."

Savalas nodded quietly as he pulled out of his parking spot.

"I'll email Savalas our report so we are all on the same page," Lopez said.

McGinnis thought he heard a bottle cap turning, but he was not sure.

"Thanks, Orlando. Take it easy on that whiskey," McGinnis said.

He heard the phone click as Savalas drove down the hill toward headquarters.

* * *

When back in his office, McGinnis grabbed a folder and opened to the section with all the information on Helen Johnson.

"We are going to have to confront this Matt Gardener and find out what his relation was to the victim," McGinnis said to Savalas.

"Do you really think she was having an affair with her former employer the entire time?" Savalas asked.

"Honestly, I have no idea. I'm sure he will have an explanation for why he continued to pay her all these years."

Savalas, who had been looking for information on Doctor Gardener on his phone, said, "Here. Doctor Matthew Gardener. Family practitioner. Married."

"I'm going to see if I can talk to him tomorrow," McGinnis said, deep in thought.

Savalas began to stir in his seat. "Something else."

McGinnis looked up.

"Emma says Marisella was jealous."

"Wait a minute. You talked to your girlfriend about the case?" McGinnis asked.

Discussing a case could be a criminal offense if anybody had anything against him. It wasn't like they didn't have enough enmeshment problems already.

"I know. I didn't tell her anything. The picture of Marisella and Helen fell out of my jacket pocket. Emma got irritated and confronted me about why I was walking around with a photo of two women in my pocket. Turns out, Emma knows them from the yoga studio. Says Marisella was jealous of Helen."

"Huh. Interesting."

Savalas nodded. "That's what I said, too. Now she's insulted because she says I'm like you, that I don't take her seriously." He sighed.

McGinnis snickered. "Sounds like we got a lot to do. How about I go talk to Dr. Gardener tomorrow, and you see to it that Farzem takes that paternity test. With Gardener, it's going to be a bit more complicated, I imagine."

"If they cooperate, chances are they have nothing to worry about," Savalas said.

"You've definitely got a point there," McGinnis said.

At least things are moving forward today, McGinnis thought, but the phone interrupted this positive train of thought. He checked the number. "It's Bartholdo." He sighed out loud. "Must want to talk to me."

"Good luck with that," Savalas said.

"Thanks, George." McGinnis sighed as he grabbed his hat from the desk and got up.

* * *

"Well, look who's here. Pasadena's most favorite detective!"

McGinnis just shook his head and didn't take off his hat. "Favorite? Really? Come on. Just spit it out. Why am I in your office today? We were just making some great progress."

"Favorite, yes. But not much longer," Bartholdo said. "Or should I use the term disreputable? I hear you were able to talk yourself out of being arrested by the County Sheriff Department, but that doesn't mean that you are going to get away with it here."

McGinnis grew quiet. He knew that once Bartholdo had a fixed idea in his mind, there was nothing he could do to change it. He silently started making plans to start a new career as a PI.

"Even though you apparently have come up with some form of alibi, your personal involvement in the case is too much."

"I'm not involved with anyone in this case," McGinnis insisted. "This is a setup. The man was shot while I was in the car with Savalas."

"I don't care what the reality of all this is," Bartholdo said. "My job here is to consider what things look like to the public. And as of right now, you are making a rather poor impression. Poor to the point of suspension, my friend."

There we go. He finally said it. I knew this was going to happen.

"Suspended? Really? Even though the facts show that I could not have done it? Why not just fire me!" McGinnis chuckled sarcastically.

"Not yet," Bartholdo said. "You're lucky Lopez doesn't have time for Pasadena. I spoke to him. He won't take it on. Meanwhile, Savalas is on the case. Sure you're happy to hear that. If I had a choice, I'd fire you. But you're too popular around here."

Sweet. So the bad news was that he was off the case, but the good news was that Savalas was on it. "Well, that's really nice of you, Chief. I'm glad I work in an environment where bosses give such wonderful, motivational speeches to their employees."

"My pleasure," said the chief.

"As for the suspension, I can guarantee you I will find out who stole my gun, and then you will see who is enmeshed with whom. And I warn you, if this is some sort of plot of yours to stop me from telling the judge that you wanted to erase Michael's body cam, you're threatening the wrong guy. You'd have to kill me to stop me from telling the truth."

McGinnis could feel his boss shrink in his soft calf-leather office chair.

In his humiliation, Bartholdo somehow managed to spit back, "I have nothing to do with this stupid case of yours. Go and figure out yourself what happened here, and don't blame me. That's your job, not mine. As for the other case, you can tell the judge what you want. He's my cousin. He's never going to rule against me."

You corrupt swine, McGinnis thought. "Well, good luck with that," he said instead.

"Find who took your gun, and we're good," Bartholdo muttered.

He seems somewhat unsure, McGinnis thought.

"But until then, you're suspended. Too much enmeshment doesn't look good."

"Fine, fine," McGinnis spat. Regardless of what an idiot he thought Bartholdo was, McGinnis knew that he had a point. The familiar faces in his case were disconcerting.

McGinnis left without another word. While walking back through the hallway of the Pasadena Police station, he wondered how he would get himself out of this mess.

* * *

McGinnis quickly escaped back into his office. He hoped nobody would tie him down with any annoying conversations before he left his desk for a few days. Nobody really needed to know any more than they knew.

Before he could set his thoughts straight, the phone rang. He picked it up and spat, "Detective."

"They found the bullet," a familiar voice said.

"Pepperstone." McGinnis sighed. He didn't know if he was happy or sad.

"It was from a Browning Buckmark Camper—"

"No way. What? I just got suspended from the case but wait a minute. A Browning?" McGinnis felt hope on the horizon.

"Yes. It's quite popular among female shooters because of the soft recoil. My wife uses one, too."

"Oh, you mean the girl," he said, and despair washed back over the detective.

"Yes, why? Did I miss anything?"

"Only a little," McGinnis said. "There's been another victim. The girl's boyfriend—or ex-boyfriend. Guess who that was?" McGinnis took a breath. He was feeling how much this case was spinning out of his control. "Alfio Cordini."

"Cordini. The guy who had the car accident with your wife?"

"Yes. The very same."

"Sounds like somebody is trying to screw you up good," Pepperstone said.

No way, McGinnis thought sarcastically. He said, "First thing you need to do, Jack, is a DNA test on Cordini. You haven't seen him yet. But he was dating the victim, so he might be the father of the baby."

"No worries, ole pal. I'll get that done. And hopefully, they'll figure out who did him in so you can get back on the case."

Yeah right, McGinnis thought. "Thank you," he said.

"No problem, ole pal. Call me if you need anything. By the way, have I told you? Lydia wants to go on a double date once this is all over."

McGinnis had to hold everything in so he wouldn't shout at his friend. "No, you haven't."

"Guess where she wants to go?" Pepperstone went on.

"I do not have the slightest clue. Tell me." McGinnis was getting impatient.

"To the shooting range," Pepperstone said, enthused.

"The shooting range? Forget that. Nell is a pacifist. She won't go near a gun. She hates those things." *I don't blame her*, McGinnis thought. His own gun had gotten him into enough trouble already.

"You have to look at it from a different angle. You have to take the violent aspect out of the shooting when practicing it as a hobby. Give her some older guns to use—some historic pieces—and show her that shooting can actually be fun if practiced responsibly."

McGinnis hadn't been at a shooting range in years, and some of the outdoor ones in LA County were a lot of fun. Maybe he would go there to practice a little on his time off. After all, he could use some practice. He used to be a good shot. He wouldn't want to miss the target if he ever needed to give his lieutenant protection. Savalas had had his back throughout the entire case already. *Time to return the favor.* He didn't really care too much about protecting himself. His weight and bulletproof vest would do that for him.

"I'll probably just go there by myself. What else am I going to do with my time off?"

"Knowing you, you'll find a way to keep working on the case."

The old coroner was reading McGinnis's mind. *It is time now to go off the record.* "Well, I'm sure as heck not going to sit around waiting to get arrested while the real culprit runs around free."

"Way to go, ole pal. I knew you weren't going to let this sit on you."

"Hell no."

After he hung up the phone, McGinnis sent a quick email to Savalas: *Victim six weeks pregnant when shot. Bullet most likely from a Browning Buckmark Camper. Who knew? Gardeners? Dr. Meyers? Wawrinski? Anyone? Who is father? Pepperstone testing Cordini body for DNA. Homicide detective suspended.*

McGinnis shut off the computer, got up, checked his still-handsome face in the mirror behind his door, pulled his hat a little lower, grabbed his phone, and left. He wouldn't bother to explain to Savalas what had happened. The email would suffice. Nor did he bother to remove anything from his office. He wasn't planning to quit his job just yet.

Chapter Ten

McGinnis went straight to Nell's. It was late in the afternoon on Monday, which was her day off. When he entered her house, he found her sitting in the kitchen, dipping an old croissant in Earl Grey tea. She was reading something on her cell phone. His unexpected arrival broke her focus, and she looked up.

"Peter?" she said.

"Yup! It's me."

"What are you doing here so early? Oh, wait a minute." She stuck her nose back into her phone, then showed it to him.

At this point, he had walked into the kitchen and given her a peck on the forehead. He took the phone. She was reading a post on an app called Nextdoor. The title of the post read: *PASADENA HOMICIDE DETECTIVE IMPLICATED? Doubts arise as case unfolds.* McGinnis stared at the words. He was taking deep breaths, trying to prevent himself from hyperventilating.

"I was just reading that," Nell said. "They are trying to blame the girl's death on you."

"W-what?" he said, then began reading the post.

Hey Neighbors,

Some of you may have been following the news on the recent murder of a released felon who had killed our local homicide detective's former wife in a car accident. The case has investigators wondering whether the newest homicide may or may not be connected to the death of the victim's ex-girlfriend, an au pair from Sweden. The case has investigators wondering whether the newest homicide may or may not be connected to the death of the victim's ex-girlfriend, an au pair from Sweden. The au-pair, whose name remains undisclosed, had been in a relationship with the victim.

According to the latest information, the girl was six weeks pregnant at the time of her death. The second victim was shot with a gun that belongs to the detective investigating the case, which has officials thinking that he may be involved. Could it be that the detective has committed a series of murders to get revenge on his former rival, who had just been set free on probation?

Authorities really should consider suspending this law enforcement official, especially since he is scheduled to testify at a court hearing on Wednesday. The hearing is a smear campaign started by a former employee of the Pasadena Police who is trying to tarnish the chief's stellar reputation.

McGinnis dumped the phone on the table. "Somebody leaked information! We don't publish information about our cases until they are solved. What is this?" He was fuming.

"Who posted it?" Nell asked naively.

McGinnis just stared at her in astonishment. *Of course. Who wrote this?* He picked the phone back up and read the name on the post: *Ramona Shelton, graduate of the Pasadena Citizens Police Academy.*

"I can't believe they didn't censor that garbage," McGinnis complained.

"It's a 'neighbor's' opinion. People can say what they want on here as long as it is not offensive," Nell said. "However, if I were you, I'd complain to whoever runs that app and tell them that they need to check posts about ongoing investigations. They should have double-checked it. Even if it's just someone's opinion."

Before they could continue their conversation, McGinnis's phone rang. He answered, spitting out, "Detective!" Then he said, "What? You again? What do you want?"

"There is a post on Nextdoor that you should see," said Zeke.

"I already know. What else do you want?"

"Just wanted to ask if you still have a job. It would be a great loss for the city of Pasadena and its citizens if you didn't."

"What? My job?" McGinnis was just about to shout back that of course he still had his job, but he came to his senses. "Actually, I've been suspended, but I don't see what any of this has to do with my car."

"Remember how I told you I'd help you if you got into a tight space?"

"No, I don't," he answered automatically. "And I don't need any help."

"You say that now," Zeke answered. "But Zeke's on your side. Remember that. And Zeke has seen this coming since he witnessed unauthorized filming of the crime scene. That was against code and was very obviously done on purpose to harm your investigation."

"Is that what you called me for? To tell me what I already know?" McGinnis asked. He was getting angry.

"Ramona Shelton. She's an old classmate of your boss's."

"Ramona Shelton, Bartholdo's classmate? How do you know all this?"

"I told you. I'm Zeke. Zeke knows stuff."

"Zeke—" McGinnis was ready to shout something indecent when he got interrupted.

"I have the yearbook. I can show you."

"How did you...? Oh, you were in Bartholdo's class?" McGinnis chuckled, but Zeke wasn't finished yet.

"Yes, and he wasn't nice."

McGinnis stopped laughing. He never laughed at people who weren't treated respectfully. "Meet me at Nell's Café at five o'clock. Oh, and bring the book. I want to see it."

"Sure, boss. See you at five," Zeke said. The phone line clicked.

McGinnis looked Nell in the eye.

"Nell's Café is closed on Mondays," she protested.

"I know," McGinnis answered. "That's why it's the perfect place. There's nobody there to listen to our conversation." He tried for a tender smile, but it came across as more of a grimace.

Nell was entirely powerless when it came to his grimace. She often told him he looked like a handsome version of Frankenstein. She stood up. "You're in luck. I have to go over there to prepare some pastry dough for tomorrow."

McGinnis checked his watch. "Oh gosh, it's ten to five!"

Nell grabbed her car keys from the hook, along with a salmon-colored cardigan. "Let's go."

* * *

When Nell and McGinnis arrived outside the café, there was barely anyone at the nearby park. They did not fail to notice the slightly shabby-looking gentleman sitting at a picnic table across the street. He watched them enter the building as he clutched a fat bundle of newspapers. As soon as they entered the café, the man at the picnic table followed suit and slipped in behind them. Nell locked the door immediately and showed them to a table in the back, where they would not be seen. She switched on the kitchen lights and the coffee machine. A few minutes later, she served the two gentlemen hot cups of coffee before going back behind the counter to work.

"Thank you," Zeke said politely.

"Don't worry about it," Nell said from behind the counter, where she was busy preparing for the next day.

Zeke began to unfold the pack of newspapers, revealing the 1980 Blair High School yearbook. He browsed through the book with a slight smile on his face, which caused McGinnis to stir nervously.

"Oh, sorry," Zeke apologized after spilling half his coffee. Luckily, most of it spilled onto the saucer.

Meanwhile, McGinnis was nearly chewing his upper lip to pieces while Zeke searched for the right page. Finally, Zeke found the ninth-grade page and showed it to the detective, who stared at it in awe. Zeke was no longer smiling, and he kept his head down as he slurped his coffee.

"Zaccharias Goldblum?" McGinnis compared the picture of the young teenager to the fifty-year-old jack-of-all-trades who was facing him. "Amazing. You still look exactly the same, except that your hairdo got even worse," he commented.

Zeke laughed. "At least I still have mine," he shot back, pointing at the photo of the then-teenage chief.

"Here he is. Bartholomew Patrick Mackenzie Meane," McGinnis said. "Fancy name."

"Wealthy, and very religious," Zeke explained. "Bartholomew means son of Talmai. Talmai is the hill or the land. Someone who carries that name is supposed to be rich or own a lot of property. Mackenzie also means something of that sort, but I honestly don't remember. All I know is that

Bartholdo was very proud of his name. He made sure that anyone who was lesser than him felt the difference."

McGinnis looked at Zeke with compassion. "I was raised by foster parents. I know what it's like to be an outcast."

Zeke looked down to avoid more emotional exchanges. Instead, he brought the McGinnis's attention back to the topic at hand. "Look!" He pointed at the photo of another classmate. "Here she is. Ramona Shelton, the glorious author of the Nextdoor post."

"For real," McGinnis said. "Why do you think she wrote that?"

"Maybe because she still has a crush on him?" Zeke guessed.

"She's not married?" McGinnis asked.

"Not that I know of. And she still has her old name," Zeke explained.

"Nowadays, that doesn't mean much," McGinnis said. "But your explanation does make sense."

"There's only one problem," Zeke said. "Your boss is dating someone else."

"Didn't know he was seeing anybody, to be honest with you," McGinnis said absentmindedly.

"Well, he is," Zeke said. "And you might want to check into it now that you're off. The issue might cause you to alter some of your witness testimonies."

"What? Who...?" McGinnis was now almost entirely at a loss.

"Fiona Sheridan," Zeke helped him out. "They're neighbors. Well, they were. More like bedfellows now," he said in a rather angry tone that sobered the detective. "Fiona was Alfio's case worker."

McGinnis did a double take. "You're serious? Fiona Sheridan?"

Zeke nodded quietly and looked down.

McGinnis began to think. *Okay, Fiona was Alfio's case worker. Zeke possibly likes Fiona. Fiona possibly ditched Zeke.* Then he stopped. "Why are you doing all this, Zeke? Are you jealous? On a revenge trip or something?" he shouted.

Nell looked across the counter with a worried frown.

"I like the sound of justice better," Zeke said plainly.

"Stop playing around and tell me what's really going on here. I have had enough of your cat and mouse games!" McGinnis ordered.

"Okay, I'll spill the beans. But it's not what you're thinking. Yes, I was dating Fiona before Bartholdo snatched her away from me. We were living together, and I was taking care of her son, whom I'm sure you know doesn't have it easy."

"You mean Max, the kid with the speaking impediment?" McGinnis made sure not to tell him that Max was the one who found the girl.

"Yes, boss."

"Did he know Alfio's girlfriend?" McGinnis asked.

Zeke hesitated for a moment.

"Did you know her?" McGinnis asked. They were now eye-to-eye.

"I can't speak for Max, but as for myself, I wouldn't say I knew her. But I knew that Alfio had a girlfriend, yes."

"How? How did you know about her?"

"From Fiona. Alfio was her case, and she felt really sorry for him. He was a lonely dude. Spent three years in jail. So he talked a lot. And I wouldn't describe Fiona as a silent mouse, either."

McGinnis was only half listening. He thought back to the interrogation on Sunday. *The mom lied to me!* He had had a funny feeling during the interrogation, but now he had it confirmed. They *did* know about the girl but had withheld that information from him. *Why? Why wouldn't they tell me that they knew she was Alfio's girlfriend? What was so dangerous about me knowing that?*

But Zeke brought him back to reality. "Do you see the connection, Detective?"

"What? Uh, no. Ahem, yes. Wait a minute. Are you trying to tell me that Bartholdo snatched Fiona away from you to get information about the girl?"

"Not about the girl. About Alfio, boss. So he could find something to blame on you. I don't know what the problem was with the girl. Maybe she knew something."

"Woah-ho, slow it down there, pal. Are you trying to tell me that Bartholdo plotted this whole thing out just to implicate me and...get rid of me?"

"You're testifying against him on Wednesday, aren't you?"

"Oh, so you know about that, too?"

"I told you, boss. I have sources. Plus, it's written in that Nextdoor post."

"Shutterbusters! You know too much. But anyway, what you're telling me is not only pointless, but it also doesn't explain who killed the victims. Or do you know that, too?"

Zeke looked down in shame. "No, boss. I haven't the faintest idea."

"Sweet. I always wind up doing the dirty work myself," McGinnis complained.

Zeke gave him a crooked smile. It confused the detective immensely, to the point that he felt compelled to take off his hat and scratch his head.

"But how on earth is it possible that it was *you* who came with the tow?" McGinnis asked.

Zeke didn't answer. Instead, he focused on a spot on the ground.

McGinnis suddenly understood. "Oh, you better not have, you pointless rascal! You did not tweak my car on purpose, did you?"

Zeke continued staring at that one spot on the ground for dear life.

"You were planning this the entire time!" McGinnis shouted at him at full volume.

McGinnis stood up, almost knocking everything over. His anger was thrumming through every vein in his body. Nell threw him a worried glance.

Zeke also stood up. He was nearly two heads shorter than McGinnis and half his size. Clearly, he was feeling lesser than McGinnis right now. As a consequence of that, or maybe to merely get out of the detective's reach, Zeke began to collect the coffee cups with jittery hands, nearly dropping everything on the floor, and brought them to Nell's counter.

"Oh, thank you, honey. That was not necessary," Nell said tenderly, which earned her a dirty look from the detective. She shrugged and carried the cups to the sink.

"Don't you try and evade me now, or I will make you feel even smaller than you are feeling right now!" McGinnis threatened him, towering over the short man like an old redwood.

Zeke looked really worried. Nell threw a warning glance at McGinnis, but he pretended not to be aware of her.

"I'm sorry, boss, but I needed you to know," Zeke said carefully.

"Stop calling me boss!" McGinnis screamed.

"Okay, boss." Zeke tried to cover his mouth, but the word had already slipped.

McGinnis sighed. "That car better come out like new when you're finished, or I will not pay you a cent," he warned.

"It will, boss. I promise. I mean, Detective," Zeke said. He quietly sighed in relief.

McGinnis was not relieved. It wasn't so much the fact that he'd been played by this amateur. He could see now that Zeke could become a helpful ally in this case. What bothered him more was the story about the girl. Was it really possible that someone would have had someone killed just to blame it on him? McGinnis doubted that even Bartholdo, whom he despised profoundly, would be capable of such a thing. And he still didn't know who had actually put that bullet in Helen's head. More would need to be done. And since there was no other information to be had, he would have to start out by asking what Savalas had gotten out of his conversation with the Gardeners, Helen Johnson's previous employers. And hopefully, the young lieutenant would cooperate even though McGinnis had lost all authority.

* * *

Zeke left Nell's Café before the detective had a chance to express his wrath. McGinnis and Nell both shrugged and, despite everything, smiled at each other.

"That dude," McGinnis said as soon as he was out the door. "I knew there was something up as soon as he came by with that truck."

"At least he's on your side," Nell said, trying to calm him down. Then she looked him deep in the eyes. "I'm worried about you, Peter."

"Aren't you always?" McGinnis shrugged her off.

But Nell wasn't buying it this time. "It's never been this bad," she said.

"That's true," McGinnis admitted. He put his hat on and edged around the counter toward Nell. "That's why I need to get going. I need to see this one through. Luckily, I got some good people on my team. Most importantly, you," he said. He put his arms around her waist and kissed her longingly.

"I love you," she said.

"Love you, too." The detective attempted to release her, but she grabbed his sleeve.

"Promise me something," she demanded.

"I'll be safe, I promise," he said, grinning. She always made him promise that before he left for work, though this time he was really leaving to save his job.

McGinnis straightened his hat and left the café through the glass door, which swung back and forth on its hinges as Nell watched him walk away.

* * *

A light wind blew around McGinnis as he walked along the tree-lined path through the playground. Leaves and debris were being blown into his path. McGinnis walked on undeterred. He pulled his phone from his blazer pocket and was just about to dial the lieutenant's number when his phone rang. The display revealed the name Pepperstone.

"Detective," he spat curiously when he answered the phone.

"Peter, that you?" the coroner asked.

"Who else do you know that answers this number?" McGinnis said.

"Nobody. Listen, Peter," the coroner said in a hurry.

McGinnis approached the courtyard on Holliston Avenue. A broken water fountain stood in the center of the untended garden. His one-bedroom apartment was located here. "I'm not going anywhere," he said. He crossed the courtyard and sat down on a cracked concrete bench, looking at the overgrown garden. It was slightly neglected but beautiful. Just the way he liked it.

"I know I'm not supposed to tell you this, but based on the characteristics of the bullet in the guy's body, it was not shot from your weapon. It was a setup. Somebody put it there to make it look like you did it. The bullet came from the same gun that shot the girl: a Browning Buckmark. That brings me to the next question."

McGinnis eyed the concrete stairway on the east side of the building, which led to his apartment on the second floor. He had been living there ever since Lauren had left him. He contemplated whether he should climb up the stairs before Pepperstone asked the question or after. Gravity prevailed. He stayed in place.

"You want to know if anybody heard shots and, if so, when," McGinnis said, helping him out.

"Always a step ahead, aren't you, Peter?" the coroner said.

"Of course. How else do you think I managed to survive in homicide for twenty-five years?"

"Well, I thought that by passing along the information, I'd ensure your existence in the police a little bit longer," Pepperstone said.

"You might have just done that. To answer your question, as far as I know, nobody heard any shots. Neither at the location where she was found, nor in her apartment. But since we're at it, can you do me a favor?" McGinnis finally rose from his relaxing position on the bench and headed toward the stairway. "Send the report to Savalas directly. Don't use my email. The chief will be opening mine. I want Savalas to see the information first. Or has Bartholdo instructed you to pass the information to him?"

"That's possible," Pepperstone said. "But I might have just had a memory lapse."

"Thank you, pal," McGinnis said. "I owe you one."

"You owe me many," Pepperstone reminded him.

* * *

McGinnis climbed up the concrete stairway two steps at a time, then headed toward the apartment at the end of the second-floor walkway. By the time he got to his door, he was panting and knew he was done exercising for the day. Still breathing heavily, he pulled out the keychain that was always attached to the first belt loop on his corduroys. He was just about to insert his key into the doorknob when he realized that someone had done that before him. The door swung open with a light push.

"Shutterbusters!" he shouted out loud. *First, they plant a gun, and then they break into my apartment? What the hell do these guys want from me?*

McGinnis instinctively slid his hand under his tweed blazer and unbuckled his holster. He opened the apartment door fully, holding his gun out, ready to fire. He entered carefully. His living room was in complete shambles. Everything had been turned over. All the contents of his chests were strewn all over the floor. He crept cautiously beside the long wall. He kicked open the bathroom door. The room had also been vandalized. Drawers and the built-in closet were open, with most of the contents scattered across the floor. A peek into the bedroom revealed that it was more or less in one piece, as there was nothing in there except his bed and a closet. The few clothes he possessed were piled up in one heap. The mattress had been pushed off the bed frame. He lifted it up with one hand and slid it back in place. Just because he was overweight didn't mean that he was not strong.

He quickly made his way to the old kitchen. While the cupboards had been left untouched, all the drawers had been ripped open. Like in the bathroom and the living room, their contents were thrown all over the floor. *Whoever was in here has already left.* McGinnis sighed and sat down on an old wooden chair. He lifted the built-in ironing board, which had been pulled out, and closed the cabinet. He looked around at the mess in his kitchen and raised an eyebrow. *What would they be looking for here if they already stole my Beretta? This doesn't make sense.* Then the truth hit him like a punch in the face.

Nearly knocking over the wiggly bistro table in his kitchen, McGinnis slowly got back up. He started to look around his living room. He made a beeline for the loveseat, lifted a couple of cushions, and pulled a Glock 19 out of the hidden slit in the upholstery. "Huh!" He almost snorted. "They didn't find this!" He checked it for bullets. The magazine was full.

He walked to the front door, closed it, and slid a fifties-style dresser made of faux wood in front of it so nobody could enter. Then he plopped onto the old woolen loveseat, removed some bullets, and aimed a blank at one of his paintings.

Bang!

Chapter Eleven

The next morning, McGinnis woke up with his gun dangling from his right hand and his cell phone vibrating on his chest. He had fallen asleep on the couch. He tried to collect himself a little before answering. Despite just having woken up, he still managed to spit, "Detective!" but his sleepy voice was a little lower and scratchier than usual, which gave away his current state.

"I'm sorry. Are you awake?" the voice on the other end asked.

"No, I am sleep talking. What's the matter, Savalas?"

"I'm ordering you back in. I read the memo from Pepperstone. Bartholdo's got nothing on you. Meet me at my office as soon as you're ready."

"All right." McGinnis let out a couple of grunts and curses while he pulled himself up from the couch. He kicked around some random items that had been thrown onto the floor by the intruder.

"Are you okay?" Savalas asked.

"Except for someone breaking into my apartment and creating complete havoc in here, getting suspended, and not making an inch of progress in my case, everything is fine, sure."

"Wait a minute. Somebody broke into your place?"

"Yes, and they did it well. I'll send you some pictures."

"What do you think they were looking for?"

In a meager attempt to clear a path to the bathroom, McGinnis began to push a pile of random things with one of his dress shoes, which he had forgotten to take off. As he plowed his way through the living room, he came across a printout of what looked like a bank statement. "Hmm," he mumbled. "Wells Fargo. That ain't my bank."

"Detective?" Savalas said.

McGinnis scanned the printout. "Ten-thousand-dollar debit on September third. Name and account number blacked out," he continued to mumble.

"Wait, what are you saying?" Savalas asked.

"Oh, yes, Savalas. Yes, well, originally, I thought they were after my other gun so they could shoot me with it and claim a suicide since their setup at Alfio's house failed miserably."

"I had no idea you already knew about the setup."

"Well, yeah, it was obviously a setup since I didn't do it. But I just found something else," McGinnis said.

"Like what?" Savalas asked, sounding tense.

"They planted a piece of evidence. Like they are trying to tell me something."

"What? Evidence? Against who?"

"Don't know. It's blacked out. I'll show you at the office."

Savalas let out a sigh of despair. "Anyway. There is more. Regarding the father."

"You found him?" McGinnis asked. He continued to plow his way through the living room, heading toward the bathroom.

"No. But we know who it isn't."

"So Farzem came and did the test without the court order?"

"Yes, he did. And he's not it."

"That's good...for him. Who else do we have? Did you talk to Gardener?"

"I did. I'll tell you about it at the office. Meet me there in one hour."

"All right."

They hung up, and McGinnis took three huge steps and disappeared into the bathroom, where he proceeded with his daily routine. When he got dressed, he made sure to put on his bulletproof vest. Just in case.

* * *

McGinnis was around the corner from headquarters, driving Nell's car, when his cell phone rang again. *Law Offices of Bob Crany Inc.*, his display read. The name faintly rang a bell in McGinnis's mind, but he could not pinpoint it.

"Detective," he spat when he answered.

"Am I speaking with Detective Peter McGinnis from the Pasadena Police?" a strong voice on the other end asked.

McGinnis held his sarcastic tongue for once. "That would be me. How can I help you?"

"I would like to speak to you about the case of Tyrone Bastille versus the Pasadena Police. You are still planning to speak in defense of Michael James?"

"I am," McGinnis said. "What's your part in this?"

"I am Bob Crany, Tyrone Bastille's new attorney." The voice on the other end waited a few moments to let this sink in.

McGinnis tried to remember where he had heard that name before. Then it clicked. "Wait a minute. Are you that lawyer guy who was on MSNBC the other day? You represent victims of police violence. Black victims."

"That's right."

"You mean you want another testimony from me? I am already scheduled to testify on Wednesday for Michael James."

"I am aware of that. And yes, that's what I am calling about. Michael James is now my case, too."

"I see. And what does that change for me?"

"We might ask you to expand your testimony. You have been at the Pasadena PD for thirty-seven years, is that correct?"

"Yes, sir. That's accurate."

"Then your current chief is certainly not the only chief you've ever worked with."

"Definitely not," McGinnis confirmed as he pulled into the parking lot on Walnut, pulling into his usual spot.

"We were wondering if you would be able to provide some insight on that in the form of a character statement for your current chief."

"You want me to say how awful he is, don't you?"

"Something along those lines," Bob Crany agreed.

McGinnis turned Nell's car off and got out. This whole Crany business made him nervous. He was just trying to get back into his job, and now somebody was asking him to assassinate his chief's character. That didn't sit well with him. He nervously glanced at his parking spot, hoping that nobody would give him a ticket since Nell's plates were not registered with the parking department.

"Well, there's nothing I would like more than doing a tell-all, but you are aware that I am currently suspended, aren't you?"

"Suspended? Why?"

"Something to do with the case I am working on. The lieutenant says I am clear, but you do understand that a tell-all against the chief might put a damper on my reinstatement."

"I understand. You don't need to tell him about it."

McGinnis grabbed his phone and looked at it, then put it back to his ear. He shook his head. "Obviously not—"

"What I was thinking of doing was preparing you for some tough questions that might come up during the hearing regarding your chief's competence. We might choose to shift focus a little from the small fish to the bigger picture, if you know what I am saying."

Yeah, I know what you are saying, McGinnis thought. *Your job is not at stake here.* "I get it, all right! But I really need to get to the lieutenant now. I already told Michael that I would testify for him. Can you just leave it at that?"

"If we leave it at that, things will never change. We are seeking the truth."

"I understand. Just ask me whatever at court. I need to go now," McGinnis said as he walked into headquarters, waving to several co-workers who recognized him on their way in. He didn't want anyone to listen in on his conversation. He'd really wanted to be done with it before he entered the building.

"No problem, Mr. Ginnis," said Crany. "Just wanted to inform you of the new situation. And please, do call me if you think you remember anything that seems significant." Crany hung up.

McGinnis popped his phone into the side pocket of his tweed blazer. *Why can't anybody say my name right.* He went up the wrought-iron stairway two steps at a time to let off some steam. By the time he was at the top, he was panting. But it felt good. He looked left and right down the hallway, hoping the dreaded chief wouldn't see him. The coast was clear, so he headed straight for Savalas's office.

* * *

McGinnis had barely opened Savalas's office door when he walked straight into the chief.

"Ah, here he is," Bartholdo said. "Speak of the devil. I see your buddy here has some evidence in your favor."

"I told you I had nothing to do with Alfio's murder," McGinnis said.

Savalas, who was calmly sitting behind his desk, interrupted the argument. "So, do we agree? Are we putting McGinnis back on the case?" he asked in an authoritative tone McGinnis rarely heard from him.

"You're back on, McGinnis. But one screw-up, and you're gone for good," Bartholdo warned him. He left abruptly, slamming the door.

"I wonder what he meant by that," Savalas said.

"It's a threat," McGinnis said. "They have the Black Lives Matter bigshot Bob Crany working on Michael's case now. He just called in and asked me to testify against the chief."

"That's interesting. I thought you were already doing that."

"Well, originally, it was supposed to be more of a testimony against Wilson. A negative character statement of some sort. It's expanded into a statement against Bartholdo Meane now. But I haven't agreed to that."

"You haven't?" Savalas seemed surprised. "After all that...crap?"

"I'm trying to keep my job, George. I happen to have some emotional attachment to it. I've been in here for almost four decades."

"Yes, I know." Savalas looked down sadly. He was not only younger than McGinnis but also more idealistic.

"How did you get him to put me back in, anyway?" McGinnis asked.

"I told him I was good friends with the head of the union and that if he didn't reinstate you, I would have them run a story on how amateur it was when he let the news team in at that crime scene. That worked." Savalas took a pen and rolled it confidently between his fingers.

"You're friends with Renaldo?" McGinnis asked, astounded.

"I am." Savalas grinned. "Old friend of the family."

"Well, whatever works." With a sigh of relief, McGinnis took his hat off and sat down.

Savalas handed him his license and weapon. "Here."

"Thanks. Tell me about Gardener. Do we need a court order for a paternity test?"

"I think so. I'm processing it right now."

McGinnis's phone started to ring, and he answered. "Detective," he spat, as usual.

Savalas just sighed and shook his head as he listened to the conversation.

"For real? Well, that sure moves things forward. I'll let Savalas know. Yeah, thanks, Jack. You, too." McGinnis hung up and turned back to Savalas. "Scratch the court order. It was Cordini."

Savalas was confused. "What do you mean? Cordini? *He* killed his girlfriend?"

"No, he's the father. He was."

Savalas shook his head again and closed the open file on his PC. "Of course. What was I thinking? Well, that saves some paperwork at least. Do we have anything else?"

"Actually, we do. Remember the woman we talked to at the horse stable near the scene?"

"Fiona Sheridan? What about her?"

"She's Bartholdo's girlfriend. Neighbors in Bungalow Heaven."

Savalas dropped the pen. "No way. How did you figure that out?"

"Sources."

Savalas gaped. "And what about it?"

"She's not the only old friend he has. Did you read the character assassination of my wonderful self on the Nextdoor app?"

"Yes. But I didn't pay much heed to it."

"By Ramona Shelton. Classmates." McGinnis slapped the 1980 Blair High School yearbook, which he had kept under his tweed jacket the entire time, down on Savalas's desk.

Savalas studied the photos. "Strange," he said, then pushed it away. "Sounds like you're a potential target. Are you wearing your vest?"

"I am," McGinnis assured him.

"And somebody broke into your apartment, you say?"

"Yes." The detective showed him the pictures. "Take a look."

"Oh, that's bad! Any clue who coulda done this?"

"I do. And I plan to pay her a visit right now."

"Who?" Savalas asked.

"The roommate. She stole my other gun."

"How do you know?"

"It's the only possibility. She took it when we interrogated her. Nobody else got so close to my leg. She did it when she picked up the cat. Must be a professional or something. She also gave me this." McGinnis slapped the bank statement down on Savalas's desk.

Savalas took the paper and read it. "You think Marisella put this in your apartment."

"Positive."

"Why?" Savalas appeared to be at a total loss. "Moreover, how did she get it?"

"I have no clue. But if you ask me, she is in the process of preparing her defense plea. Did you check her background?"

"I did. There's nothing on her. At least not since two thousand fifteen, when she moved in with Helen. But she's at least forty, I would say, so there must be more."

"Coulda had her record sealed," McGinnis said.

"It's going to take me a moment to get access to that."

"All right, then let's add a search warrant. About time we took a closer look at the victim's home environment, don't you think?"

"Sure. I can get that started. What do we do meanwhile?"

"I want to talk to Matthew Gardener. Maybe he would know something about the bank statement they dropped at my place."

"Do you need me there?"

McGinnis put his hat back on. "No, I think I can handle that."

"All right. Then I will make sure we get that warrant ready."

"Great! I shall see you in the afternoon," McGinnis said. He left the lieutenant's office, swaying as he walked.

* * *

McGinnis was unable to suppress his joy over his reinstatement at his job. He strode toward Nell's car, swinging his long legs swiftly, taking even bigger strides than usual. He whistled a tune, then stopped abruptly when he detected a parking ticket stuck on the windshield. "I can't believe this. First, they try to fire me. Then they give me a parking ticket when I'm parked in my own spot!"

He whisked the ticket out from under the wipers and strode back toward the main entrance of the headquarters building. He was no longer whistling. He barely waited for the semi-automatic, solid wooden door to open before he made a beeline for the clerk behind the glass wall.

"Hey, this is my assigned spot. You can't write me a ticket for my spot!" McGinnis complained when he arrived at the desk. There was a line of people waiting for the clerk's attention, but he had entered through the employee door.

The clerk appeared embarrassed. "Are you aware of any reason they might have written this ticket?" she asked diplomatically.

"Well, I didn't come in my usual car. Mine's in repair."

"Well, there ya go, then," the clerk said. She distorted her mouth into something that resembled a smile. "If you come with a new car, you have to register it with us. Otherwise, the parking attendant thinks it's someone else's." The clerk handed McGinnis his ticket back. "Sorry!"

McGinnis fumed. This day had started out so well, and now this. "But it's not a new car! This is only temporary—"

"Doesn't matter," the clerk said. She had already summoned the next person to her counter. "The parking attendant cannot tell the difference."

"No, they can't, because they're idiots!" McGinnis mumbled. He grabbed his parking ticket, which amounted to fifty-five dollars, and stormed out of the building.

When did the police become horse thieves? McGinnis wondered as he strode back to his car, heavily pounding his heels into the ground.

* * *

If McGinnis was good at one thing, it was dismissing a random matter for the more important issue at hand. Hence, he got in his car, carefully folded up the parking ticket that had caused him so much frustration and placed it in his battered wallet before typing his destination into his GPS. *1269 Mar Vista Ave, Bungalow Heaven. Here we go again,* he thought, remembering the many times his investigations had led him to this much-desired neighborhood full of twentieth century Craftsman bungalows. *Everything looks so fine, but then you have the people who live in them.* It wasn't that he could not have found the address on his own—McGinnis knew the Pasadena area inside and out—but the GPS made it easier to find a specific house number.

He drove for a while and finally arrived at Mar Vista Ave. The very popular green patch of McDonald Park, which was situated on his left was more brown than green. It was mid-September, and the only reason the grass was not entirely scorched was because of a sprinkler system that operated daily.

The neighborhood had finally come up with the funds to install much-desired floodlights, a community issue that had been on the table for almost a decade. As he calmly rolled up Mar Vista Ave, which was well shaded by the ancient oak trees hanging over the sidewalks, McGinnis did feel some relief that there was at least a tidbit of sanity in his hometown.

His navigational device led him to an appealing two-story classic Craftsman bungalow. He made a U-turn and parked the car on the curb next to a nicely landscaped front yard—most of it was a greenish-yellow semi-burnt-up lawn that was probably impossible to keep green due to the current water restrictions. A row of various-colored roses surrounded a spacious front porch that was mahogany-stained. A mix of concrete and brick stairs led directly to the front door, which was elegantly carved and appeared to be from another period.

McGinnis walked up and rang the brass doorbell. He heard steps nearly instantly. A well-dressed woman around his age, wearing casual navy-blue slacks and a white blouse, opened the door. Like him, she was slightly on the heavy side and appeared to be sweating. If it weren't for the expensive clothes, she would look just like any other suburban mom.

"We are not buying anything," she said, nearly closing the door in his face.

McGinnis took out his badge and showed it to her. "Pasadena PD. My name is Detective Peter McGinnis. Are you Mrs. Gardener?"

"Oh, I see," the lady said in a cool tone as she stood in the door-frame. "One of your people was here yesterday. I'm so shocked to hear what happened to Helen. But I'm afraid my husband is not going to submit himself to any paternity tests. There is no reason to. It is also rather insulting."

"I am very sorry we made you feel uncomfortable, Mrs. Gardener. But in homicide, we cannot afford to be polite when we conduct an investigation. We have to simply take all possibilities into consideration and operate strategically. However, I do have good news for you. The paternity issue has been resolved. We no longer need Mr. Gardener to do the test."

"Oh, thank God!" Mrs. Gardener said as she continued to stand in the door. "That was so...offensive," she repeated. "Why... What do you need from us now?" There was a slightly nervous shake in her voice, which indicated discomfort with the situation.

"I was hoping to speak with your husband, actually. It appears that until recently, the victim was receiving a salary from him even though she hasn't worked for him in years."

"Oh, that's explainable. She was doing his taxes. Helen Johnson was an expert accountant. When my children no longer needed a nanny, Michael hired her as his accountant for his medical practice."

"Is that so?" McGinnis asked. He shifted from one leg to the other, as he was becoming increasingly uncomfortable standing planted in front of the door. The sun was shining directly on his head. If it hadn't been for his hat, his scalp would probably be getting sunburnt. Sweat was running down his forehead. It must have been at least a hundred degrees outside.

"That is so," McGinnis heard a male voice say in the background. "Rose, why don't you ask the gentleman from the police in," Matt Gardener said. He was standing on a polished step of the stairway leading to the next floor.

"Oh, yes, of course," Rose Gardener said half-heartedly. "Come on in." She finally opened the door to let McGinnis in. "Would you like a glass of water?"

Seems embarrassed, McGinnis thought. "I cannot turn that offer down in this heat," he said.

When McGinnis stepped inside, Matt came down the stairs and extended his hand. McGinnis instantly felt better in the coolness of the air-conditioned hallway.

"Matt Gardener, MD, PhD. I believe I met a co-worker of yours yesterday."

"Peter McGinnis, homicide detective. The gentleman you are referring to is my colleague Lieutenant George Savalas. A very good man."

"He most certainly made a good impression on me. However, I had nothing to do with Helen's pregnancy, as I understand you now know. I am a very faithful husband. Rose and I have been married for over thirty years," Matt said.

Rose came back with a glass of ice-cold water, which McGinnis chugged down in one go. Matt put his arm around Rose, and they stood like that as if to prove how well they got along. McGinnis handed the glass back, unimpressed. *Posers.*

"Thank you, Mrs. Gardener. Ice water works miracles in this heat."

Rose took the glass. "My pleasure, Mr. Ginnis," she said, then headed back toward the kitchen.

"McGinnis, that is," he corrected her.

Rose ignored him.

"May I suggest you join me in my office?" Matt said. "I would like to enlighten you on Ms. Johnson's role in my family."

"Sure."

"Come along."

Dr. Gardener led McGinnis through the cool entryway, where the light was dim due to Tiffany windows. *Originals, of course.* They went through a living room with old maple-wood floors. The fireplace was covered with gray-green tiles, some of which had hand-carved imprints of oak trees and other nature motifs.

"Those Batchelder tiles?" McGinnis asked.

"Yes, Mr. Ginnis. A lot of the materials in this house are still the originals. We have spent many years returning the house to its original state, and our home has been selected to be part of the Bungalow Heaven Home Tour Day three years in a row."

Good for you, McGinnis thought apathetically. "McGinnis, that is," he said out loud.

A watercolor painting of a scene at the beach hung over the fireplace. It had some similarities with Kenton Nelson's New Realism paintings. However, the artist appeared to have some trouble with the figurative elements of the style.

"That's not a Kenton Nelson over the fireplace, is it?" McGinnis asked just to be sure.

"Oh, funny. Everybody asks that. No, it's my wife's. She's a painter in her own right."

"Oh, I didn't know that."

"No problem, Mr. G— I mean, Mr. McGinnis. You can't know everything. Here we are."

The tall and good-looking Dr. Gardener had led the detective to a side room on the south side of the house. The room apparently served as his office. A large and old-fashioned mahogany desk was placed in the center of the room, in front of a group of bay windows situated over a group of built-in cabinets that matched the maple floor. The desk was resting on a burgundy Persian carpet, which complemented the dark maple wood perfectly. *Original, of course.*

Dr. Gardener made a beeline for the cabinet, where he pulled out a folder labeled *Helen Johnson*. "Please, Mr. Ginnis, have a seat."

"McGinnis," the detective defended himself one more time.

"Of course, McGinnis. I am sorry."

McGinnis sat down in an antique Chippendale chair, while Dr. Gardener sat in a more modern, pompous leather office chair.

"Here is the situation, Mr. McGinnis." Dr. Gardener emphasized his last name on purpose. He kept his hand on the folder as if it were worth a bar of gold. "As you surely know, Miss Johnson worked many years for us as a nanny. She came to us from Sweden directly."

"Yes, Dr. Gardener, I am aware of that."

"Good." Dr. Gardener began to fumble with the folder but then stopped. "During her time of service to our family, I became aware that she had a previous degree as a bookkeeper. Even while she was still taking care of the children, she helped me out in the practice once and a while. It turned out she had a fabulous grasp on numbers. I had her go over the billing that the medical assistant put in, and she often found mistakes. Do you follow?"

"Easy to follow, of course. And then when your kids were old enough to take care of themselves, you hired her as a bookkeeper."

"Well, that's not exactly what happened. Originally, I had no intention of hiring her when we saw that the kids were going to be fine on their own. We were just going to send her back to Sweden or dismiss her. However, then I got the offer to teach at UCLA. That changed everything."

"Just how?"

"You would think that being a professor is an easy job. Long vacations. Assistants to correct the papers. Just a couple of hours of teaching here and there."

"I have no idea. I have never been a professor. You tell me," McGinnis said. This guy was beginning to bore him. *So full of himself.*

"It wasn't easy at all. The few hours of teaching I thought I was required to do turned out to be a job with overtime. I had to oversee an administrative committee. I had to prepare lessons, write syllabi, and, first and foremost, research. Oh, and the practice, of course. As one of the major pediatricians who observed the development of immunity after giving antibiotics to children, I had a big audience to inform.

"Basically, I was writing research paper after research paper, going from conference to conference. I had no time to control the finances. I hired

Helen as an accountant the year after I got hired as a professor. Here is the entire history of our work relationship. I let her go this year when I decided to close my practice." Dr. Gardener pushed the Helen Johnson folder across the desk to McGinnis. "You can borrow it for the time being. Just promise me you'll bring it back in one piece when you are done. We are all very sad about what happened to Helen, you know. She was a dear person to us."

"I see," McGinnis remarked coolly. "Just out of curiosity, where was your wife in all this, if I may ask? Does she have a career of her own that required her to have support at home?"

The question caught the successful doctor somewhat off guard. He pondered for a while. "No, actually, my wife just likes to do projects of her own. She's a highly talented painter who needs the time to herself. I support her that way. She has had many exhibits over the years."

"I see," McGinnis said. He had his hand on the folder and had been browsing through it absent-mindedly. He closed it abruptly. "Would you mind showing me exactly where I need to look in order to see when her time at your practice started? We have a lot of files to deal with every day. Some oversight helps."

"Of course. No problem." Dr. Gardener took the folder back and opened to the first page, where the neatly organized table of contents was.

McGinnis stood up and walked around the desk to look over his shoulder. The folder looked new. *Looks like he just put this thing together yesterday.*

"You see here in the front that there's a section labeled *Johnson 1269 Mar Vista*. In this section, I have listed the salary that we paid her when she worked for us as a nanny. And here in the next section, *Johnson 1136 East Green Street*, is when she began working at my office in 2015."

"Your practice was at 1136 East Green Street?"

"Yes. I was there for over thirty years."

"Nice building," McGinnis said. "My doctor also has his office there."

"It was the perfect place for a doctor's office," Dr. Gardener said. "Smack in the middle of the city."

"I understand," McGinnis said. He'd had quite enough already of the Gardener family's history. "One more question. Where are your kids now, if I may ask? Off to college?"

"Yes, Mr. Ginnis," Dr. Gardener said, reverting back to the wrong name. "My son, Archibald, is studying to be a chemist at Cornell University in New York, and my daughter, Audrey, studies English literature at Stanford."

"Impressive," McGinnis said. "You've got quite the perfect family, haven't you?"

"Thank you. Yes, my family is my pride and joy."

McGinnis grabbed the folder. "Wonderful," he said. "Then that's about it. I appreciate you letting us borrow the information for the time being. Savalas, the colleague of mine you met the other day, will make sure it gets returned to you in the same perfect state that you lent it to us in."

"I'm not worried at all," Gardener said. "Let me show you out." He stood up and led McGinnis out the other door in his office, which led to the driveway.

"So long," McGinnis said as he stepped out and lifted his hat. The heat smacked him like a bulldozer.

Why on earth can't anyone ever get my name right? he wondered as he walked back to Nell's car, which was now at least twenty degrees hotter than before.

Chapter Twelve

McGinnis didn't bother stopping for lunch. He had no appetite in this heat, not to mention the fact that he was too busy.

He had a hunch that Savalas was still in the same exact spot where he had left him that morning: his desk. He parked Nell's car in the very spot he'd gotten fined in that morning, but this time he wrote down the license plate number. Again, he walked through the majestic semi-automatic entrance and into the public area of the department. The hall was busy, so he took the side door into the administrative section and went directly behind the counter. A different clerk—this time someone he was vaguely acquainted with—sat there now.

"How you doing, Detective?" Jordan Koenig, the young black clerk, asked. He had just finished serving one of the customers on the other side of the glass.

"All's well here. Only, I was wondering if you could forward this plate number to the parking attendant. I'm driving a different car than usual."

"Sure. What happened with the old Futura? You got rid of it or something? That car was cool!"

"No, I still have it, but it's in repair."

"Awesome that you're keeping it. I really like it." Jordan looked at the note. "You know, normally there is a form you need to fill out, but don't worry. I'll handle it for you."

"Thanks, Jordan. I'd appreciate if you could handle it right away. They gave me a ticket this morning because I didn't notify them."

Jordan grabbed the aluminum closed sign and slid it in front of his window. The customer in line complained.

"I'm sorry. Next window," Jordan said to her unapologetically.

The woman cringed and joined the other line.

"They gave you a ticket for parking in your own spot?"

"Yes, and the clerk who was there this morning thinks I'm going to pay for it."

"No, you're not," Jordan told him. "You won't get ticketed unless it goes into the system. I can find out who worked in parking and have them throw out the ticket before it gets processed."

"Appreciate it, Jordan. I'll remember that," McGinnis said. "Don't forget to give them my other plate number. I don't want this to happen again." He was already heading toward the stairs.

"Don't worry, Detective. I got this," Jordan said.

McGinnis took the steps to the second floor two at a time and headed straight into Savalas's office. He knocked carefully on the half-open door.

"Come on in!"

As he had assumed, the lieutenant was sitting in the exact same spot he'd been in earlier.

"You do realize that you have not budged since I left this morning," McGinnis teased him.

"That's possible. It's not like I haven't done anything, though." Savalas turned around in his chair and grabbed a piece of paper from the printer. He handed it to McGinnis, who was still standing in the same spot.

"The search warrant?" McGinnis said incredulously.

"Yep!" Savalas said proudly.

"How did you get it so fast?"

"Judge Wagner had no hearings this morning, so I was able to catch him in his office right away. It took a little persuasion to make this a priority, but he finally signed the damn thing."

"Oh man, George. You really make things happen around here!"

"I'll take that as a thank-you. How did your conversation with Dr. Gardener go?"

"Great. Another one of those people whose life is close to perfect. Except his wife's artwork. She needs a little more practice."

"His wife is an artist?"

"Yes. Apparently, she likes Kenton Nelson's style. Or at least, that's what the painting over the fireplace looks like."

"Don't know who that is."

"He's one of Pasadena's finest. Been around for decades. His work has been shown in museums all over the world. You probably know his Colorado Bridge work. I've seen it many times on the covers of Pasadena-related books at Vroman's."

"No clue," Savalas admitted.

"You should look him up some time," McGinnis suggested.

"So, what about the Wawrinski lady?" Savalas brought them back to the point. "You still planning to pay her a visit, or what?"

"Oh, yes, man, sure. I just...did not expect you to be ready so soon."

Savalas just sat there and smiled.

"So what are we waiting for?" McGinnis said.

"You not gonna call and see if she's there?"

"Not if I can avoid it. Nothing like surprising a suspect who knows something."

"We bringing anybody along?"

"Not at the moment, no. I just wanna see how she responds. We'll call the people in to search the place once we've confronted her."

"Great, then. Let's go. I am getting cabin fever from sitting at this desk all morning."

Savalas got up, and together they left the office.

"You drive," McGinnis ordered as the two cops hurried down the hallway.

* * *

For the second time, McGinnis and Savalas stopped in front of 1097 East Orange Grove.

McGinnis glanced up at the window and noticed a moving curtain. "She's there!" He tapped Savalas on the shoulder.

"How do you know?"

"The curtain."

Savalas looked up and saw it moving. "We better hurry, or she might try to get away," he said.

Savalas and McGinnis quickly rushed up the steps. Savalas was quicker than McGinnis, who was panting, but he kept up well.

Savalas knocked. "Hello, Ms. Wawrinski. Pasadena PD. We have more questions."

Silence.

Savalas tried again. "Ms. Wawrinski. Pasadena PD. Please open the door."

Nothing.

"Ms. Wawrinski. Open the door! We have a warrant!"

Clang! The sound of a thump caused Savalas to stop. The two cops looked at each other.

"That came from the back," McGinnis said. "Go! You're faster than me!"

Savalas stormed down the stairs, prompting the tenants on the lower floor to peek out their doors. "Pasadena PD," he shouted as he bolted out of the building.

McGinnis leaned on the old wooden door, then took a step back and rammed into it with his full weight, which was an easy thing for him. The door crashed to the ground with barely any resistance, and he walked in and stood in that square-shaped hallway. Again, he had the sensation that something was missing. Then he became aware that the door and window were open. He entered Marisella's room. Clearly, she had been planning to leave town, as a half-packed suitcase was on her bed.

McGinnis looked through the open window and watched Savalas chase after Marisella. She had apparently climbed out onto the rooftop, then climbed down to the ground, when she saw them coming in through the front. She was a couple of yards ahead of Savalas, but he had an easy time catching up with her, as he was in great shape. All at once, though, she stopped and shouted, "Stop! Or I will shoot you," unaware that McGinnis was watching her from the window.

He pulled out his reacquired Sig Sauer and pointed it at her from the window. "I would not do that if I were you, Miss Wawrinski. I may not be a good runner, but I am a sharp shooter."

Marisella hesitated, then shouted, "Nonsense. There's no way you can get me from that distance—"

She was correct, but McGinnis's trick had worked. Savalas approached her slowly and then tackled her during the fraction of a second that she was distracted by McGinnis.

"You're under arrest for threatening a law enforcement officer. You have the right to be silent!" McGinnis heard Savalas say as he handcuffed her.

"Take her to headquarters," McGinnis shouted out the window. "I will have a look around here."

Savalas gave him a thumbs up as he walked the reluctant young woman to the car. McGinnis watched a neighbor on North Michigan Avenue, who was watering the front yard of his Craftsman bungalow, curiously turn his head and watch them walk down the quiet street.

McGinnis stepped away from the window and turned his attention back to the suitcase, where he discovered an open Browning Buckmark Camper protection case. The gun was missing, of course. He immediately took a picture of it with his phone and sent it to Pepperstone with the message, *Would this weapon fit any of the bullets?*

Then he texted Savalas and said, *We need to get a forensics team asap*, thinking to himself that there had to be more than just an empty gun case in the place.

While he was looking around Marisella's perfectly tidy room for more evidence, Shadow came out of nowhere and snuck up next to McGinnis's leg.

McGinnis looked down. "Oh no. Not you again. Get away from me!" He gently pushed her away and started to sneeze as she arched her back. Carefully, he pulled a folded cotton handkerchief from his breast pocket and blew his nose.

Except for the suitcase, there was not much to find in Marisella's room. It was all clothes and shoes. *Clearly, she was not planning to stay here for long*, he thought.

He decided to have another look at the square hallway that had always disturbed him. He entered and focused on the floor. He noticed that the yoga mats had disappeared, and everything was clean. The wood floor had been freshly oiled, it seemed. *Would anyone really polish a floor after their friend just passed?* he wondered. He kneeled down and checked the floor around the edges of the wall and near the chairs. The wood planks closest to the wall were clearly lighter than the ones in the center. The difference in color revealed a distinct line. McGinnis started to follow the line around the room, but then he bumped into a pair of legs.

"Detective McGinnis?" the legs said.

McGinnis looked up. "You're from forensics, aren't you?"

The face that belonged to the legs nodded.

"You have to excuse me. But I believe I just found a piece of evidence. Missing evidence, rather. What is your name, please? I recognize you from the other scene. You helped me with the tweezers," McGinnis said as he stood up.

"William Barnes, forensics." The forensics officer pulled his wallet out of his breast pocket and showed his ID.

"McGinnis," the detective said.

"I know," Barnes answered as two more workers came up the stairs with suitcases. "They are with me."

McGinnis sighed. "All right then. Since we're at it, can you see the slight discoloration of the hardwood floor around the edges of this room?"

"Looks like sunlight stains. Probably had a rug on the floor at some point."

"Very good," McGinnis said. "Do you think you can find some fabric, see if it matches what we found at the scene?"

"Ah, I see what you are saying. Yes, of course. If this was recent, definitely."

"As recent as Saturday. Has been polished over, though."

"Oh, then definitely. No problem."

Shadow entered the square hallway and started meowing.

"Who does she belong to?" one of the female workers asked.

"The suspect. She's in custody right now. Wanna take care of her while we deal with the suspect?" McGinnis sneezed again. "I think I'm allergic."

"Sure," the woman said. "I'd love to. Does she have a name?"

"Shadow." McGinnis sneezed again. "And you?"

"Marion Jackson," she said, then started cooing at the cat, who arched her back and ran out the door. "Oh no! She ran away."

"Just like her owner," McGinnis said sarcastically.

Marion shrugged and taped off the door.

"I would like to know if this could be the scene where it happened. We are looking for blood samples, most likely on one of these walls here. The killer was a sharpshooter. Most of it was cleaned already. It's very possible it happened here, though, because I think they rolled her in the rug after they killed her."

McGinnis saw a spot on the west wall near the entrance. "Like this here. Could this be blood splatter? I see a bunch of these spots with my bare eye. Take samples, please. And the other walls, too. You know what I mean. I'll go downstairs and talk to the neighbors while you look around, okay?"

The forensics examiners went to work while McGinnis went downstairs, knocked on the first door, and said, "Pasadena PD. Is anyone here?" He heard feet shuffling and whispers.

"Yes?" a middle-aged female voice said.

"I just have a couple of questions regarding your neighbors from upstairs," McGinnis said. He tried to play it down so he wouldn't scare the people.

"Oh, they mean the Swedish woman and her girlfriend," McGinnis heard a male voice say, and then he heard the sound of a chain being removed. The door opened carefully.

McGinnis had his license ready and showed it.

"Homicide?" an older man in boxer shorts asked, clearly intimidated.

"Yes, unfortunately."

"Who died?" the woman whispered. She was wearing a bathrobe.

"Must be the Swedish one," the man, most likely her husband, answered. "The other one was here this morning."

"Is that true?" the woman asked.

McGinnis evaded her question. "Actually, I wanted to ask you if you'd heard anything. Any shots, noises, or banging. Anything suspicious."

The middle-aged couple looked at each other.

"I'm not sure. I heard a thumping sound one night, but I don't know. Mathilda, when was it that we woke up in the night?"

They looked at each other again, uncertain.

"Saturday night," Mathilda said.

"How do you know it was Saturday?" McGinnis asked. "Do you remember anything specific?"

"Saturday is date night. We went to Buca di Beppo and came home at about ten o'clock."

"Oh yes, that's right. It must have been Saturday. Remember when I woke you up and you said, 'That sounded like something from one of those shows,' Tildy?"

"Hugh likes to watch *Dateline* on Friday nights. You know, that show about the murders. I don't like it, but Hughey watches it all the time."

"So Saturday," McGinnis noted. "That is very helpful, thank you. Can you remember what time it was?"

"It was about one o'clock in the morning. I looked at the clock. Remember, Hughey? I said, 'It's the middle of the night. Let's go back to sleep.'"

"Yes, only I didn't go back to sleep. Takes me a long time when I wake up like that. Thought I heard some voices and shuffling afterward, but I didn't think much of it. They're young people, and they make noise all the time. Especially on the weekend."

"I see," McGinnis said. "Did you hear any fighting? Any arguments, yelling, shouts?"

The couple looked at each other again and shook their heads.

"No, nothing," the man said.

"What about a shot?"

They both thought for a long time, then shook their heads again.

"No, we didn't hear any shots. Only the thumping, the shuffling, and the whispering," Mathilda answered.

"All right then, Mr. and Mrs....?"

"Norton," they answered.

"Does this mean we are getting new neighbors?" Mrs. Norton asked.

"Again!" Hughey sighed.

"I can't tell you that. If you do, I hope you get nice ones."

"Yeah," Mathilda said.

"Thank you," McGinnis said, then left.

In a hurry to confirm a hypothesis, McGinnis went back upstairs, taking two steps at a time. Marion saw the panting detective when he came to the door of the apartment, so she took the tape off one side, let him enter, and put it back on.

Barnes was busy spraying luminol onto the wall that McGinnis had pointed out, and he addressed McGinnis excitedly, saying, "Detective! Look! You were right. We found the marks on the wall. They look like they're from a gunshot."

"I can see that," McGinnis said, but he rushed past them. "I'm sorry. I have to check something in the suspect's room."

He went back into Marisella's room and rummaged through her luggage. Sure enough. A silencer. This woman was a professional. Savalas was going to have to get an order to open her background file.

A few layers under the clothes in her suitcase, McGinnis discovered an envelope. He opened it and found ten freshly printed Grover Clevelands. He dropped everything and immediately went back into the hallway, where the forensics people were busy taking samples.

"I need a baggie," McGinnis ordered. "And gloves."

Barnes was quick to hand him the necessary items. "Here. Anything else you need?"

"Come with me!" McGinnis walked him into Marisella's room and showed him what he had found. The clothes from the suitcase were in heaps all over the bed. "Sorry. That was me. I was looking for this." He put the gloves on, grabbed the silencer, and put it in the baggie. "Here!"

"A silencer?" Barnes said. "Who is this? Some secret agent or something?"

"I have no idea. But I'm about to find out."

"That's wild," Barnes said as he took the baggie.

"There's also a case for a Browning Buckmark that you might want to secure, and there's ten thousand dollars in an envelope. Just to be safe, I have photos of the original state of the suitcase."

"Looks like somebody was on the run," Barnes remarked.

"Yes. But too late. Savalas caught her. Guess where I'm headed now. Any questions?"

"No, sir," Barnes said as he began the process of securing the evidence.

"Oh yes, one last thing. The other room is the victim's room. Make sure you preserve all papers, especially photos. We will be going through her bank statements and employment records. Personal stuff."

"No worries, Detective. We'll have it all ready for you."

"Thank you, Barnes," McGinnis said, then left the room.

In the hallway, he ran into Marion, who lifted the tape again for him.

"Thank you, Miss Jackson," McGinnis said, lifting his hat off his head.

"My pleasure, Detective," Marion said as she stuck the tape back on.

Chapter Thirteen

Savalas greeted McGinnis in the hallway on the second floor of the Pasadena PD building. McGinnis was panting after his two-step ascent. Savalas looked distressed.

"What's the matter?" McGinnis asked him.

"Oh, nothing. Marisella's in the interrogation room. She's one tough cookie. Won't say a word. Maybe you'll have more luck."

"All right, do me a favor," McGinnis said. "Start the process of getting her background unsealed."

"You found stuff?"

"Silencer and ten Grover Clevelands. She's been paid. Question is by who."

"Consider it done," Savalas said in a rush before hurrying to his office.

McGinnis entered the interrogation room, where Marisella was sitting at the end of a long conference table. She was wearing all black. *Stunning woman*, McGinnis had to admit to himself.

He took off his hat and sat down at the other side of the table. "What were you doing in my apartment?" Marisella gave him the stink eye.

"I know you're the one who took my Berretta when we interrogated you the first time. You're the only person who came near it. As for my apartment, there is nothing to steal in my place except weapons. Why didn't you take one?"

Marisella continued to stare into the void.

McGinnis banged his hand on the table. "All right. Let's try this from another angle. Who paid you?"

This time, Marisella appeared caught off guard. She nervously grabbed a brown curl and started to chew on it, then tossed it away half-headedly.

"Ten thousand dollars is not exactly a lot of money nowadays. I can't imagine it's worth it to kill your best friend for that much, especially considering all the trouble it gets you in," McGinnis said to her.

"She was *not* my best friend," Marisella said.

"Oh, so now we're talking. Let me guess. She had the wrong boyfriend?"

"She never loved Alfio. She was only using him. I told him that many times. As soon as she found someone with money, she dropped him."

"What are you implying? That she was dating Farzem?"

"She would have if she had lived longer, the slut. But he was way too careful. His wife guards him like a puppy dog. And those were not *my* words."

The detective was a little surprised. "Helen said that?"

Marisella nodded.

McGinnis decided not to let her distract him from the real issue.

"Did you know that she was pregnant?"

Marisella reflected for a moment. "She mentioned it."

"Did she tell you whose it was?"

"The Farzem guy, most likely. What do I care? Let me out of here. You got nothin'."

"Actually, it was not his. Alfio was the father. And I do have something. We searched your apartment."

Marisella did not look at him.

"Let me take another guess. You knew that, too."

Marisella briefly glanced at him, then looked at the observation window.

McGinnis began to get angry. "You know, there is one thing I cannot stand, and that's when somebody has an issue with someone and they try to make it look like it's mine. Who paid you?"

Marisella nervously glanced at the observation window again. "I don't have to answer anything without a lawyer."

"That's correct, Marisella. You do not. And let me tell you something else. You will need one very soon because it's only a matter of time until we figure out who gave you the ten grand."

Marisella stared at him with big eyes. "You went through my things?"

"Yes, dear. We told you at the door that we were coming with a warrant. We found the money and the silencer. You're a professional. Somebody hired you. And sooner or later, we'll find out who."

"You had no right to go through my things! I want a lawyer."

"Don't worry. Nobody took anything. What bothers me more is this." He slapped the bank statement from his apartment down on the table.

Marisella looked nervous.

"Why did you put it in my apartment?"

No answer.

"All right. I will tell you why you put it there. You planted it because you knew that sooner or later you were going to get caught. What I don't understand is how you got your hands on it in the first place."

Marisella snickered.

McGinnis was getting increasingly angry. "Don't think that I did not see that snicker!" he shouted, almost beside himself.

At that moment, the door to the interrogation room burst open. It was Bartholdo. McGinnis quickly grabbed the bank statement and stuffed it in his tweed blazer.

"What are you doing in here, McGinnis? Harassing innocent people?"

"Harassing, maybe. Innocent, no. Who told you she was here?"

"Nobody. I happened to stop by."

McGinnis grumbled. He knew that Bartholdo was in the right for once, and there was not much he could do. "I see. Well, take off, then, Miss Wawrinski," he said calmly as he put his hat back on.

Marisella looked from one to the other and slowly stood up. "What? You're not arresting me?" she asked, dumbfounded.

McGinnis sent her a warning glare. "Not today."

"Smith!" Bartholdo screamed.

Officer Smith appeared instantaneously. "Yes, Chief!"

"Escort this young lady out."

"Yes, sir." Smith walked Marisella out of the interrogation room.

"And you. I would like to have a word with you," Bartholdo said.

"Go ahead. I'm not going anywhere."

"If I catch you pressuring innocent people into making confessions one more time, I will fire you!" Bartholdo shouted angrily, and then he left the room.

McGinnis watched curiously as the chief disappeared around the corner. Then he grabbed his hat and went to find Savalas in his office.

* * *

"You know, that was strange," McGinnis confessed as he sat down in one of Savalas's extra chairs.

"What do you mean, strange? You were getting a bit loud, weren't you?"

"Why would *he* care about my exact procedures? Him, out of everyone? I mean, look at his record. He doesn't give a damn if anybody gets hurt."

"Maybe because of the court case, he's being extra cautious."

"I guess that's possible. What about her background? Have you made any progress?"

"Actually, I have. We owe Wagner a huge favor."

McGinnis rolled his eyes. "Let's hear it."

"Served twenty-five years in State penitentiary. She was in the Navy before that. First degree murder. Apparently, it was a revenge act. Guy from her troop tried to rape her. Or raped her. She was never able to prove it. She got out in two thousand fifteen."

"Who was her parole officer?"

"Fiona Sherridan."

"What?"

"Fiona Sherridan."

"But that's... She's Bartholdo's girlfriend!"

Savalas stayed very calm. "She the one at the horse stables?"

"Yes! The boy's mom! Remember? We talked to her."

"Strange how everyone seems to know everybody, but nobody knows anything about the case."

"Don't worry. I'm starting to see through it. At least part of it."

"You think Fiona told Bartholdo about Marisella, and then he hired her?"

"Possible. Or someone else."

"But that doesn't make sense. What does Bartholdo have against Helen Johnson?"

"Nothing."

"And how does that explain Alfio's murder?"

"Well…"

"All those murders just to accuse you?"

"Maybe it's not me. Maybe it's the girl they didn't like. It seems she had a habit of stealing other people's husbands. Or at least, that's what Marisella thinks."

Savalas considered. "You mean Matthew Gardener and Farzem?"

McGinnis lifted his left shoulder in an attempt at a shrug. Instead, he got it stuck. "Aw shucks."

"You all right?"

McGinnis quickly massaged his shoulder. "I think I just got something stuck. But I'm fine."

Savalas rolled his eyes. "How do you suggest we proceed, then?"

"Bank accounts. Somebody took out ten Grover Clevelands in cash. That someone can tell us why Helen Johnson had to die. *And* Alfio Cordini. I also want to put a forensics guy on this." McGinnis pulled the bank statement out of his tweed jacket. "You think they can figure out what it says under the black Sharpie marks?"

Savalas studied the printout. "Don't know. Definitely worth a shot."

McGinnis gave it to him. "Keep the original and make me a copy. I have a hunch I'll be needing it."

Savalas stuck the statement under his printer and put the copy on the desk. "What did Marisella tell you?"

"Oh, she did not like Helen. Was jealous of her and Alfio. They could probably relate to each other with both of them having been in prison. But that doesn't give her enough motive to kill Helen. Not after serving for twenty-five years."

"Wait a minute. Maybe it does. She did once before kill for revenge. Why not do it again?"

"Revenge murder because Helen dated the guy you had a crush on? After twenty-five years in prison? That's quite different from getting raped."

"I agree. Highly unlikely. So where is she now?"

"Bartholdo made me release her."

Savalas did a double take. "She's running around free even though we found evidence in her apartment? And after she threatened to shoot me?"

"Trust me, it's better this way. She won't do us any good behind bars. If she's still waiting for the rest of the money, chances are she's going to stick around."

"Okay, well, I guess I have to trust you on this one."

"Not like you have a choice. Bartholdo won't let us keep her."

"All right. What does that mean for me?"

"You take care of the legal stuff."

"So, bank accounts..."

"Yes."

There was a stretch of silence.

Savalas nearly whispered, "*Whose* bank accounts?"

"Leslie Meyers. Dr. Farzem. Matt Gardener. Matt Gardener's wife. And Bartholdo, of course."

"Bartholdo..."

"Yes, the chief."

"And *how* do you suggest we obtain those records?"

"Subpoena, of course."

"And you think they're just going to grant us that without any internal investigation."

McGinnis took off his hat. "Not right now, no. We would have to prove everything first."

"Then what do we do?"

"I have an idea."

Savalas looked at McGinnis with big eyes.

"The lawyer's name is Bob Crany," McGinnis said as he put his hat back on and started fumbling with his phone. "The Black Lives Matter guy."

"Tyrone Bastille's lawyer," Savalas added.

"Exactly."

"When did you say your court case against Bartholdo and Wilson is?"

McGinnis stood up and scrolled through his phone contacts. "Tomorrow."

Savalas shook his head and sighed. "Why does everything always have to be in such a rush?"

"I would say that maybe things are just finally starting to come together," McGinnis answered with a half-smile. He swept up the copy of the bank statement and stuffed it back into his pocket.

"Wait a minute," Savalas protested. "Didn't you want that checked by forensics before you go out and about with it?"

McGinnis had already left his office. "Not the copy!" he shouted back from the hallway.

Chapter Fourteen

Nell had stopped by earlier to pick up the car, so McGinnis decided to walk home, at least part of the way. He wanted to get some fresh air. Plus, he could always get an Uber if he decided it was too far to walk.

What's with Zeke and my car, anyway? Is he ever gonna finish it? McGinnis had his hand on his phone to call him, but then he decided not to bother, preferring to take in the cool breeze on the autumn night.

It was around seven PM, but there was still daylight. Soon, the days were going to get shorter. The civics center of Pasadena always filled him with a sense of peace, for he was a firm believer that no matter how bad things got, in the end law and order would prevail.

He took off his tweed blazer, rolled up his sleeves, and threw the blazer over his left shoulder, all the while keeping a steady pace. It felt good to just move instead of thinking, thinking, thinking.

No, I'm not calling Zeke today. I've had enough of him for a bit. I have a better idea. McGinnis pulled his phone from the side pocket of his blazer. He dialed a number.

"This is Bob Crany," a voice answered promptly.

Not bad. A TV personality who actually answers his phone, McGinnis thought. He attempted to keep the spit in his mouth as he answered, "Detective McGinnis here. I was wondering if you had a moment to talk—"

"I knew you would come 'round," Crany said.

McGinnis grumbled a little. He never liked it when he was the one who had to give in. "Where you staying?" he asked the lawyer.

"I'm at the Westin, right next to the courthouse. Shouldn't be too far from where you work," Crany said.

"I'm coming right around the corner, actually. You're at the hotel this moment, you are saying?"

"I am! Why don't you meet me in the lobby? I'll come down from my room."

"Sure. See you there." McGinnis hung up. He loved it when things went his way. That was what he was used to.

* * *

McGinnis entered the carefully uncluttered lobby of the Westin Hotel. Several transitional style sofas helped some overworked hotel guests convert their high stress levels into relaxation. The detective made a beeline for the desk, where a perfectly groomed hotel clerk greeted him with a rehearsed smile.

"How can I help you, sir?" the pretty Latina lady asked.

"I'm supposed to meet a Bob Crany," the detective said.

"You want me to—" The gentle lady was interrupted by an audible clearing of the throat.

"Right behind you," a deep voice said.

McGinnis turned around and saw the face of the man who was changing America. To McGinnis, he looked no different than any other man, except for his figure, which was fitted into an expensive suit, was more imposing, as if the heavyset lawyer was trying to make a point by merely standing there.

McGinnis shook Bob Crany's hand. "Nice to meet you in person."

"My pleasure."

A bunch of chattering hipsters around thirty years old came through the hotel door, slowed down, and whispered when they saw Crany. They stared at him as if he were a statue.

Mr. Crany pulled McGinnis aside. "May I suggest we find a more private location? I am already getting too much attention down here," he explained in a low voice.

"What are you thinking?" McGinnis asked trustingly.

"Had any dinner yet?"

"No, actually."

"Then how about we go to the restaurant? There's a pizzeria right near here. The people will still be staring, but at least they won't be sharing our table," Crany said, managing to squeeze out a smile.

McGinnis couldn't care less. He would certainly not refuse food, though. "Sure, let's go there."

"All right."

* * *

It was clear from the moment they entered California Pizza Kitchen, just a block down from Westin, that Bob Crany had already made arrangements prior to their arrival. The waiter on staff ushered him right to a table that was slightly removed from the main crowd in the popular restaurant.

"This is a little better. Nobody knows I'm here, so we shouldn't be bothered."

The waiter brought them water and the menu.

McGinnis, who was thirsty from the short walk outside, emptied the glass in one go. "How did you know I was coming today?"

Crany was studying the menu, but he looked up and gazed at McGinnis over the rim of his glasses. "I didn't. But I was hoping you would." He focused back on the menu, which seemed to interest him more.

Interesting guy, this Crany. Keeps it all in like a pro. I've always been the other way, wearing my emotions right on my sleeve. Speaking of sleeves... He pushed up the sleeve that had fallen over his elbow. It had cooled down considerably since the afternoon, but it was still hot.

The waiter came and took their order. Crany went with a light tomato pasta, and McGinnis chose the creamy chicken Alfredo dish. He was starving.

Once the waiter was gone, Crany no longer had the menu to hide behind, so he addressed McGinnis with reluctance. "What you got for me? You ain't here to socialize, I presume," he said, wiping his face after taking a sip of iced tea.

This guy is right up my alley. Does not mess around. "I need bank statements."

Crany put down his iced tea. "What?"

"Bank statements. From three people. Well, five, really. Some of them are most likely joint. We can make arrangements to get four of them. The problem is the fifth one."

Crany started to snicker. "And who would that one account belong to?"

McGinnis and Crany looked at each other. One may have thought they were having a staring contest.

"Bartholdo Meane."

Crany's deep laughter shook the table. McGinnis's water almost spilled.

"Get outta here!" Crany shouted, then kept on laughing. He eventually calmed down. "Any other wishes?"

"No," McGinnis said, which caused Crany to gape at him open-mouthed.

Crany eventually broke into another fit of laughter.

"I didn't realize I was so funny," McGinnis said.

Crany's laughter ran out, like a motor running out of gas, as he continued to stare at McGinnis's plain face. He took another sip from his unsweetened iced tea. "And how am I supposed to get those statements?"

The waiter brought their plates.

"Ah, food!" Crany sighed.

They began to eat.

"I thought that since you're on Michael James's case, you might be able to help. Look." McGinnis pulled the bank statement out of his jacket and put it on the table.

Crany studied it. "Somebody withdrew ten grand. And?" he asked, chewing heartily while studying McGinnis.

"That's the ten grand we found in the suspect's suitcase today. We believe she was paid to get rid of, well, at least one of the victims."

Bob Crany began to chuckle. "Ten grand to kill someone? Who agrees to that? That amount is ridiculous. Are you sure it's that?"

"Almost positive. It would help to know who the person was who paid it. We believe the rest was supposed to come after."

"Oh, I see," Crany said. "And what would my role be in this?"

"One of our suspects is Barthold Meane. I can't obtain his bank information unless the department launches a formal investigation. Considering the sensitive nature of the situation, an investigation of that sort could backfire."

"Badly, yes," Crany said. He chewed heartily and studied McGinnis like a work of art.

McGinnis explained himself. "I thought if the subpoena came from outside the department, it would not cause such a stir."

Crany continued to stare.

"Hey, this was not my idea," McGinnis defended himself. "You are the one who asked me about Bartholdo's record earlier today. Here I come with an item, and you are laughing in my face." He rolled a huge portion of alfredo onto his fork and stuffed it in his mouth.

The two heavyset guys faced each other, both chewing.

"Somebody paid a former convict ten Grover Clevelands to shoot a victim and her lover. The lover happened to be my ex's lover, as well, before he killed her in an accident. I know Bartholdo would love to see me hang for killing Alfio." McGinnis paused and took a sip of water. "It was either one of the victims' employers or Bartholdo." He had momentarily stopped eating in order to speak, but now he took another bite.

Crany swallowed. "I heard about that. Alex Cardone?"

"Alfio Cordini."

"Poor fellow."

"Indeed."

"You are basically offering me something about Bartholdo that's not on his record yet." Crany took another bite.

McGinnis said, "The idea is to have the information on his record before trial. I mean, if that is what really happened."

Crany considered for a long moment. "Show me that bank statement again."

McGinnis pulled it out of his pocket again and let Crany study it.

"It could be a fantastic piece of evidence if it turns out to be the chief's. Unfortunately, I don't have any legal reasons to subpoena it. I'm afraid you are going to have to get it some other way."

McGinnis stuffed it back into his pocket. "Yeah, that's what I was afraid of." He was unable to keep the disappointment from his voice.

"And you think that it's all been a setup to stop you from talking tomorrow?" Crany asked.

"That's not even where I was going with this, but it's definitely one of several possibilities." McGinnis ate the last bite of his alfredo.

Crany finished his pasta and asked, "What are the others?"

"Adultery. The victim apparently had a taste for other people's husbands."

"How does that explain the Cordini death?"

"It doesn't," McGinnis said. He took a sip of water to wash his down.

Crany stared at McGinnis. "If you want me to get a subpoena for Meane's finances, I'm gonna need something more concrete than that. You know that, McGinnis." He wiped his mouth clean.

"I am aware of that," McGinnis said, copying Crany's move. "However, I thought you might've wanted in on my latest findings."

"Shoa," Crany said.

When the waiter returned to the table, Crany asked for the check. McGinnis made a motion to cover his own tab, but the famous lawyer shrugged him off and said, "This one's on me," as he signed the check.

McGinnis began to put his blazer back on. "Thank you."

"So you showin' up tomorrow, Detective?"

"Sure I am," McGinnis said. He stood up and reached out for a handshake.

Crany shook his hand. "An' let me know if you make any progress on that Cordoni case and his gal's," he said.

Together, they walked toward the door.

"Cordini," McGinnis corrected him.

The hostess held the door open so they could exit into the concrete courtyard, which seemed to emit all of the heat it had absorbed during the day. McGinnis put on his hat and turned right on Colorado Boulevard. Crany turned left, heading back to the Westin.

Chapter Fifteen

McGinnis's apartment was over a mile away. So was Nell's house. He decided to walk so he could digest the carb-loaded dinner he had just enjoyed. After all, Pasadena was McGinnis's hometown, and it was rare that he got to spend time in it. The evening was pleasant as shoppers chased after the latest deals and patrons entered restaurants for a special ambiance.

I can understand why people would want to work with that Crany guy. He seems to be competent, McGinnis thought to himself as he rapidly strode along the classic Route 66, his blazer casually swung over his shoulder. Then his phone rang. Of course, it was Savalas.

"Any news?" the best of lieutenants asked when McGinnis answered.

"Boy, you don't ever stop, do you?"

This must have confused the conscientious lieutenant, because there was a long silence on the line.

"I just thought I'd ask about those subpoenas," Savalas said.

"We can always get the Meyers and the Gardener ones. Farzem, also."

"No luck with the other one?"

"None."

"So what do you suggest?"

"Change of strategy."

"What?"

"Even if we get the statements from all the others, they can appeal the subpoenas. That would make it a lengthy process."

Again, there was a long silence. All McGinnis could hear was the sound of papers moving on an office desk.

"What do we do?"

"Let *her* show us."

"Who? Marisella?"

"Yes. Ten grand is not a lot for two jobs. She's waiting for the rest of it. Why else do you think she's still here?"

"And how...? You mean, I have to send someone to keep an eye on her?"

"Not you."

"So what do I do?"

"Go home to your girlfriend. Take a break. You've done enough. I got this. You can start ordering those subpoenas first thing tomorrow morning."

"You have your court case tomorrow," Savalas protested.

"Exactly!" McGinnis said. He was already breathing heavily. The heat did not make the walk easy. "That gives you plenty of time to get the paperwork started. You know how much I don't love paperwork."

"Right," the lieutenant said. "Well, let me know how it goes."

"Sure thing," McGinnis said before hanging up and putting his phone in his pocket.

The warm evening breeze felt good on McGinnis's skin, which was not used to fresh air. And the walk made him feel at least three pounds lighter. *Why don't I do this every day?* After about a mile or so, he passed Lucky Baldwin's on Colorado, his former go-to spot when he needed some space to think. He hesitated for a moment in front of the entrance but then decided not to go in. *Aw, I'll just walk home.* The air felt really refreshing, and he knew that no drink on this earth could compare to fresh air. So he continued straight ahead on Colorado Boulevard. Then he pulled his phone out of his blazer's pocket again and dialed a familiar number.

"Yes, boss! It's boss! I was wondering when you would call. Your car is running again. I'd only need your permission to give it a coat of paint."

"I'll have to think about that, Zeke. It's probably going to cost a buck or two..."

"Oh, for you I'll make a special price. Won't charge you for the work. You'll only have to cover the paint, the spray gun, and the sander..."

"Like I said, it will cost me a buck."

"Come on, boss. It will look like new."

McGinnis had arrived at Michigan Avenue, so he turned right. "Listen, Zeke. That's not what I'm calling about. You can paint it if you want, but you'll have to discuss the color with me first."

"Of course, boss! I would never touch your car before checking with you."

I'm not so sure, McGinnis thought, moving the phone to his left hand, as his right hand was sweaty from all the walking. He had covered over a mile on foot today, which was quite the achievement for the old sluggard.

"Enough of that now. Listen. About your offer—" McGinnis switched his phone back to the other hand.

"Four thousand!" Zeke shouted down the line.

"Not that," McGinnis said. However, he was not at all surprised to hear a big number. He slowed down to cross at a traffic light on Green Street.

"It's a really good price for all the work I have put in. Your car is going to run like new. And look it, too. However, it does not include the paint."

What a shrewd little thief! McGinnis thought. He was getting unnerved. "Zeke. Now listen. Are you still in on that favor you mentioned?"

Zeke was suddenly suspiciously silent. "Favor? Favor? What favor?" he asked nervously.

"Come on now. You can stop acting. You said you would help if—"

"Yes, that's true, boss," Zeke immediately corrected himself. "What do you want me to do?"

McGinnis got a green light and crossed. "All right. So the victim's roommate. Or do you know who that is, too?" He strolled down Michigan Avenue, now heading toward Nell's house.

"Roommate? Victim? I don't know anything, boss."

"Of course you don't," McGinnis teased him. "Anyway, I'm gonna need you to keep an eye on her. Write this down. Marisella Wawrinski. 1097 East Orange Grove, Pasadena. See who she hangs out with, talks to, etcetera. Somebody gave her a lot of money, and it's not all of it. And we're gonna need to catch her before she runs away with it."

"You know your car is gonna take longer if I have to go tail your suspects now. Can't you get someone from your department to do that?"

McGinnis slowed down for a moment and chuckled. *Who is this dude, anyway? First, he offers help, and then he doesn't want to do it!* "Are you gonna do it or not? Because if you're not, I'm gonna have to do it myself, and that would be difficult because she already knows who I am, man."

"Sure! No problem, boss. I'll be on it in five minutes. Just need to get my camera and my car ready. Been working on yours all day."

"1097 East Orange Grove. Upper apartment. I'm assuming she's not leaving town, because someone still owes her for the Monday morning Altadena job."

"What? She killed that one, too?"

"That's what we are thinking, yeah. Now you got your info straight from the source."

"I sure did!" Zeke sounded excited. "What do I do if the person who owes her the rest of the money shows? Stop them?"

"Hell no! Just call me asap."

"All right." Zeke sounded a little disappointed.

"Make sure you record it if you see anything. We're gonna need proof if we want to nail down the one who paid her."

"That's a done deal, then, McGinnis. What do you think of red?"

But the detective hung up.

Chapter Sixteen

McGinnis walked several blocks south on South Michigan Avenue. The street was completely quiet. The busy hustle and bustle from Colorado Boulevard had disappeared the farther east he had walked, the residential zones nearby quiet. Nell's little white Craftsman was on the west side of South Michigan. As McGinnis passed Steuben Street, he looked up at a deep red, orange, and purple sunset.

Nell's car was parked neatly under the carport, as usual. McGinnis approached the front door and decided to ring the doorbell. *She has no idea I am coming. I don't want to frighten her.* It was almost dark, after all.

Absentmindedly, McGinnis picked a piece of white paint off the peeling wood on her house. *When this is all over, I'm going to hire a painter for her.*

He was deeply absorbed in his thoughts when the door opened a crack and a frowning Nell carefully peeked through. She was wearing the same bathrobe she wore whenever she got comfortable at home. Her left hand was stuffed in the pocket of the robe.

McGinnis immediately recognized the crease between her neatly groomed eyebrows. "What's wrong?" he asked her softly.

Nell said nothing. Instead, she grabbed his hand and pulled him into the house, immediately closing and locking the door. McGinnis tossed off his shoes while she hooked the chain back on.

"Come with me!" she ordered, pulling him toward the kitchen by his hand. He had just enough time to toss his hat on the Thonet rack.

As they entered the kitchen, the kettle began to whistle. Nell quickly rushed to the stove and shut it off.

"You have a visitor," Nell said bluntly as she began pouring the tea.

Fiona Sheridan was sitting in the corner of Nell's rustic built-in kitchen nook. She had exchanged her plaid work shirt for a simple t-shirt and jeans. Her freshly washed wet hair was hanging loose.

"Fiona Sheridan?" McGinnis said incredulously.

Nell placed a hot cup of tea in front of Fiona. Fiona briefly glanced at McGinnis, then looked at her hot tea, which she gratefully picked up and sipped on. She put the teacup down and still said nothing.

"Do you want a cup of ginger lemon tea, Peter?" Nell quickly came to the rescue, most likely sensing the tense atmosphere.

"Nah. I just walked all across town. Tea's too hot for me now. Let me just grab a glass of ice water."

McGinnis was about to take a glass out of the cupboard, but Nell was faster. She held it under the automatic water dispenser on the fridge and handed it to him, saying, "Here!"

"Thanks, love." He gave her a confident peck on the cheek.

McGinnis drank the water down in one go and banged the glass onto the table. He somehow managed to squeeze his bulkiness between the bench and the table as he sat down, and he let out a huge sigh of relief.

"How can I help you, Miss Sheridan?" He was almost content now that he was back in Nell's house.

"Just call me Fiona, okay?" she said, almost annoyed.

"Sure, Fiona. So what brings you here? Wait. Let me guess. Something to do with your current boyfriend?" McGinnis said. He glanced at Nell as if to check whether he had impressed her with his provocations.

Nell offered him an angry frown.

McGinnis raised an eyebrow and focused on Fiona instead.

"Go easy on her, Peter," Nell admonished him. She grabbed his glass and filled it up with more water.

McGinnis looked Nell in the eye. "Thank you, love." He kept looking at her. With a movement of his head, he motioned for her to give them some privacy.

Nell understood. "I have some laundry to do. Call me if you need anything." She looked at Fiona. "If you will excuse me." She left the kitchen, closing the door behind her.

"All right. I apologize if I was being a little tense before," McGinnis began. "But I have had my license suspended, had my apartment broken into, been accused of murder, and had my car break down. And one of your boyfriend's classmates thought she had to assassinate my character on the Nextdoor app. That was all a bit much, and we are not even halfway through the week."

"Ramona Shelton. Blair High School. Bartholdo's old classmate. Has a huge crush on him. I think she would lie down in public and kiss his feet if he asked her to," Fiona said dismissively. She took a sip form her tea.

"Yes, so I've heard. But what does that have to do with you?" McGinnis took a sip from his ice water.

Fiona looked him straight in the eye. "Promise me something."

"Let me guess. You want this conversation to be off the record."

Fiona's tense expression loosened up a little. "I was hoping it would be that way, yes. You know, since Bartholdo and I... I would not want him to know that I am speaking with you about this."

"All right. We can keep it that way for now, but only until the case gets solved. I might need to get some form of official testimony from you once we go to court with it," McGinnis explained. "You think you can live with that?"

"Yes, I guess. As long as he doesn't know that I came here, that's fine," Fiona said. Then she looked down into her teacup. "I lied to you." She lifted her gaze. "In the horse stable. You know, when you came and talked to Max."

Interesting. Not that I didn't know that already, though, McGinnis thought. "You knew Helen. You knew that they were dating—or had been—and you also knew that she was pregnant. And so did Max. Is that correct?"

Fiona looked at McGinnis, then quietly nodded and looked down again. "Yes, it's true. But we had no idea... I mean, he asked a lot of questions, and I thought it was strange. But I did not think much of it. Maybe it's all a coincidence. But when Max came back and told me about the body that morning, I broke up with Bartholdo the same day. I just... Something was off. And then Alfio!" She sighed, and a tear rolled down her cheek. "He was doing so good! The guy should never have been in prison in the first place."

"Wait a minute. You broke up with Bartholdo the day they found Helen? Why?"

"Like I told you, something was off. He kept asking questions about Alfio that he had no business asking. It's like he was investigating him or something." Fiona paused and looked at McGinnis angrily. "Now don't think what I think you are thinking. Bartholdo did not do it. He would never... At least, I don't think so. He is not capable... But I don't understand. He was so into the whole story. He kept badgering me about Alfio. Wanted to know where he was working, who he was dating. He even asked where his girlfriend lived." She shook her head. She had been speaking increasingly erratically.

"A question, Fiona," McGinnis said. "Were you also Marisella Wawrinski's case worker when she got out?"

Surprised, Fiona picked up and then put down her teacup. "Yes, I was. But that was almost seven years ago."

"You know that she moved in with Helen Johnson about half a year ago?" McGinnis asked.

Surprised, Fiona said, "No, I did not know that. I mean, I believe I may have heard Bartholdo speak of her in some context, which I did find strange at the time, but I did not pay much mind to it. It is a strange coincidence, yes."

"Question. When she got released, did she have some sort of special deal where she would have her record sealed?"

Fiona pondered over it. "Hmm. It was a long time ago, but I don't think so. She was quite the distinct character, and I think I would remember such a thing about a case, even after all this time. I can go through my files and check for you if you want," she said. "To make up for lying to you on Sunday." She finished her tea and looked up.

"That would be very helpful. Yes, please do that. Now, about this. Did you come here to tell me that you are sorry for lying to me, or is there anything else you would like to tell me?"

Fiona looked at him with big eyes. "Well, yes, and well, I kind of already told you. I just wanted to come clean, yes. And, well, let you know that I thought that Bartholdo's behavior was odd. Kind of off." She looked down, and McGinnis could have sworn he detected another tear rolling down her cheek. "I think he was using me. He was not really into me. He wanted something, but I am unable to pinpoint what. All I know is that once Max found Helen, I'd had enough. And so I thought...it would be a good idea to tell you since you are the—"

"I understand. Well, I am very glad you came. Else you would have heard from me or Savalas very soon."

"And you promise this stays between us?"

"This conversation will not go on the official record. Bartholdo won't know. Do we need to worry about your safety?"

Fiona shook her head vehemently. "No, no, I'm fine. I can take care of myself. Bartholdo is my neighbor on Bell Street. It would look funny if there was a police car surveilling me. Besides, I'm not afraid. It sounds like *you* should be!" She stood up.

At that moment, Nell quietly opened the kitchen door. "Sorry, I just need to get a screwdriver. The tumbler is loose again," she said as she opened a drawer.

"Ah, we were all done here, anyway, weren't we, Fiona?"

"Yes," she said. A smile of relief appeared on her face.

Nell smiled back at her and then at McGinnis.

"Let me walk you to the door," McGinnis said, and he escorted Fiona out of the kitchen. "One question." They walked across the old hardwood floor of the hallway, which so desperately needed to be polished, and headed toward the entryway. "How did you know to find me here?" he nearly whispered. "As far as I am concerned, Bartholdo doesn't know anything about my private life." They had reached the entry hall. McGinnis opened the door.

Fiona picked up her pocketbook and turned around to face McGinnis. "Zeke. He told me."

"Darn it, Zeke. Of course he told you! How could I not have thought of that?" McGinnis scolded himself.

Fiona grinned and walked out. "I'll call you tomorrow if I find anything on Marisella," she shouted across the crispy front lawn as she headed toward her car.

"Sure! And tell Zeke I would like to have my car back some day."

McGinnis closed the door and walked back into the kitchen, where Nell was waiting for him. She was sitting at the kitchen table, sipping a cup of tea. He sat down beside her and let out a huge sigh of relief.

"Everything all right, Peter?" she asked.

"Yeah. I'm really glad she came out on her own."

"She looked rather relieved when she walked out of here. You should have seen her when she knocked at the door! I thought she was going to confess to the murder or something," Nell said.

"No, it was not exactly like that. But the conversation was very helpful."

Nell looked at her wristwatch. "Gee, it's almost nine o'clock. Isn't tomorrow your big day at court?"

"Yes, it is. And I do not look forward to it."

"We had better go to bed, then. You don't want to show up there all tired and grumpy."

McGinnis shrugged, and they got up and went to bed.

Chapter Seventeen

Bob Crany winked at McGinnis when he walked into the courtroom early the next day. Crany was standing in front of a man in a wheelchair, whom McGinnis immediately recognized as Tyrone Bastille. Crany was bending down, obviously explaining something to his client. McGinnis noticed a tiny old black woman sitting immediately behind Tyrone. She wore a hat and a dress with a mixed floral pattern on it. *Must be the grandma.*

McGinnis got almost all the way up to the front before he noticed Michael James sitting in the same row as the black lady. He went over to the wooden bench and said, "Hey, Michael, how's it going?" He extended his hand.

Michael, a fiftyish, slightly heavyset man, took his hand and held on to it for a moment before standing up. "Thank you so much for doing this, Peter," he said, embracing him.

McGinnis hugged him back. "No problem, man. A good man deserves a good word for his great work."

Crany walked up to them. "Come on, Detective. Let me introduce you to my client and his family. Let's start with Mrs. Bastille, Tyrone's grandmother." He turned to the woman. "Mrs. Bastille, this is the detective I have told you about. He is going to help with Tyrone's case."

The tiny little lady looked up from under her hat and said nothing. She stared at McGinnis's face as if it were a statue. McGinnis tried to break the ice by extending his hand. She did not take it, though.

"Thank you," Mrs. Bastille said. She looked straight ahead at the court.

Crany shrugged the awkward moment off. "Come. Let me introduce you to my client."

McGinnis clumsily followed Crany to the front of the room.

Crany walked up to Tyrone, who was poring over a document. "Tyrone, this is Detective Peter McGinnis from the Pasadena Police. He is our witness today."

Tyrone looked up. McGinnis was staring into the face of a young kid—eighteen, maybe—his life just barely started. While looking into this young kid's face, the entire series of events that had occurred over the past week began to flash through McGinnis's head, as if it were all happening just now. It was as if the whole world had stopped and frozen when McGinnis caught sight of this kid who would be a paraplegic for the rest of his life. And it was all because one guy at his workplace had a bad temper.

Tyrone extended his hand. "Nice to meet you, Detective. Thank you for coming," he said.

Tyrone's words tore McGinnis out of his momentary frozen state. He gave Tyrone his hand. "Of course. I'm sorry this happened to you," he said. But somehow, his apology felt ridiculous in the face of the burden this young kid would have for life.

Tyrone said nothing. He just looked at McGinnis with big eyes and withdrew his hand.

The door at the front of the room opened, and the bailiff, a court reporter, and some security personnel stepped out and took their places at the front and center of the room. Bob Crany sat down next to Tyrone in the front and advised McGinnis to take a seat in the same row where Michael James and Tyrone's grandmother were sitting. McGinnis entered the bench on the right side and sat down next to Tyrone's grandmother so that he would not have to stand up when it was Michael James's turn to speak from the witness stand.

McGinnis noticed Fred Wilson walk through the door. It seemed to McGinnis as if Fred was throwing him an angry glare. However, the exchange was interrupted when Fred's lawyer caught up with him and advised him to take a seat in the front on the left side. A young woman of South Asian descent sat in the row behind them. *Let me guess. That's the girl who was working at the shop when it happened*, McGinnis thought as he finally sat down.

McGinnis observed Tyrone's grandmother raise her head high as she watched Fred Wilson. It was as if she was daring him to look at her. *Probably doesn't even see her*, McGinnis thought. He was beginning to take a liking to this fierce little lady who had refused to greet him even though he was speaking in her son's favor.

The last person to arrive was Barthold Meane, who snuck in like a thief.

Once Fred Wilson and his lawyer were sitting down, the bailiff stood up and said, "All rise."

Everybody stood up. The judge finally entered the courtroom. He put down a folder and glanced from left to right, then looked straight ahead.

The bailiff went on, saying, "The court is now in session."

Finally, the judge took over. "Everyone be seated."

That judge sure does not look like a relative of Bartholdo's to me, McGinnis thought as he studied the judge. *I wonder whether he was wrong about which judge would be assigned to the case.* Then he glanced over at Bartholdo, who looked tense.

After some formalities, the judge opened the trial. "At this time, the prosecution may begin their opening statement," she said, making herself comfortable in her seat.

Bob Crany stood up. "Honorable Judge, sadly I stand here in front of the court—once again—for a case of police brutality against a black male. While fortunately the plaintiff was not killed, he *has* suffered a severe physical injury to his body. As a consequence of the encounter at a Seven Eleven store, where the officer Fred Wilson of the Pasadena Police responded with an excessive and unnecessary display of violence, Mr. Tyrone Andrew Bastille is now paraplegic, tied to a wheelchair for the rest of his life.

"Let me be clear. Tyrone is well aware that his behavior was out of line when he complained to the store assistant, Miss Shilva Patel, who is sitting to our left here, about somebody cutting the line. Yes, it is true that Tyrone let her have it for serving the white customer before him even though it was his turn. Yes, Tyrone Bastille can see now that he should not have called her a racist slut. He is sorry for that. Shilva would not have needed to call the police in the first place if Tyrone Bastille had just been quiet, paid for his groceries, and left the store."

Crany had been pacing up and down the front of the courtroom. He stood still for a moment, took a sip of water, and went on. "And yes, if I were Shilva's father, I would have also told her to call the police." He glanced at Shilva, who was probably not more than twenty-five years old. "However, that does not explain—it does not justify, and it does not make it right—the way that Tyrone has been wronged by the Pasadena Police. Mr. Bastille is now a paraplegic, tied to the wheelchair for the rest of his life, at a time when his life had just begun!"

Crany motioned for the judge to look at Tyrone, who tried to maintain a cool demeanor despite the attention on him. Mary Bastille, Tyrone's grand-mother, shook her head.

"And yet here he is. A nineteen-year-old man—or should I say kid—whose life is ruined because, once again, a policeman could not keep his temper in check." Crany stood still, gazed at Fred Wilson for a moment, and then went on. "And why? Because he raised his voice? Because he stood up against a man who was disrespecting his place? Because he refused to be silent when, once again, his rights as a shop patron had been taken away? And even if he was wrong—even if you think, Honorable Judge, that he should have been quiet and just waited his turn—the punishment for speaking up is undeserved.

"He may have verbally attacked Miss Shilva, but he did not physically assault her, nor did he destroy or steal anything. Instead, he was physically assaulted by the police. In an entirely inappropriate move, even though Tyrone kept saying repeatedly that he was 'unarmed and did not do any-thing,'—and in spite of Mr. Michael James, Fred Wilson's colleague's, repeated requests to stop—Fred Wilson made Tyrone kneel down, and then he kicked him so hard in the back with his steel-toed boot that the damage was instantaneous.

"There is nothing, Honorable Judge, that excuses such excessive violence in a simple store conflict. It is for this reason that Mr. Tyrone seeks the rightful punishment of Mr. Fred Wilson, who was violent in a situation that could have been resolved peacefully. After you have heard all the evidence,

Your Honor, we will ask you to proceed with this trial." Crany, who was finished with his statement, sat back down.

"Thank you, Mr. Crany. The defense may begin their opening statements now," the judge said.

Stacey Miller, a thin, slick man in an expensive-looking, tailored blue suit, stood up. "Honorable Court, Honorable Judge, this is never going to become a trial. What we are all experiencing together is just one more example of the defamation of a hard-working member of the Pasadena Police. He was risking his life to maintain peace during a situation of high conflict.

"Mr. Fred Wilson did not use excessive force. When his patrol got called in during a high-stress situation after the defenseless shop assistant, Ms. Shilva Patel, called for help, he was merely doing his duty. When Mr. Fred Wilson entered the shop on Rosemead Boulevard with his colleague, he witnessed a man who was out of control. Mr. Bastille had been shouting incessantly at Miss Patel. Meanwhile, the patron who had apparently offended him had already left the store. Nevertheless, Mr. Bastille continued to threaten Miss Patel verbally from across the counter. Please note, Honorable Judge, that the plaintiff in question measures a full six-foot-two when standing upright and is of considerable physical strength.

"When he saw the patrol team enter the shop, he lost control entirely and attempted to flee. Mr. Wilson and Mr. James drew their weapons and blocked the door. Tyrone Bastille ignored Fred Wilson's repeated orders to put his hands in the air. Wilson told him to kneel down. Again, the suspect did not follow orders, so Mr. Wilson gave him a nudge in the back of the knee. Tyrone finally knelt down with his arms behind his head. However, Mr. Bastille did not stay that way. Tyrone slowly and nearly unnoticeably began lowering his left arm toward his belt. Mr. Wilson, who was worried that he was going to draw a weapon, needed to stop him while keeping him in check with his own drawn weapon, which he was holding with both hands.

"Mr. Wilson used his foot to stop Mr. Bastille from getting anywhere near his belt. It was a gentle nudge. If Mr. Wilson's attempt to prevent the plaintiff from gaining access to a weapon resulted in him using slightly more force than intended, it was due to the stress that the plaintiff should not have put him under in the first place. However, the gentle nudge that Mr. Wilson gave the plaintiff was nowhere near the harmful kick that the prosecution describes. We therefore believe that Mr. Bastille either had a previous back injury that he did not disclose to the prosecution or, even worse, he is faking it. But Mr. Fred Wilson's gentle nudge was not capable of creating the type of injury we are sitting in court discussing today. Therefore, Honorable Judge, I trust you to dismiss this case, which is nothing more than nonsensical and defamatory to the good reputation of Officer Fred Wilson."

"Very well, Mr. Miller. The court thanks you. You may sit down," the judge ordered.

Stacey, who had gotten heated during his speech, walked back to his place while shaking his head. When he went to the defendant's table, Fred Wilson gave him a high-five. McGinnis shook his head in disgust.

The judge addressed Crany. "You describe a situation involving police violence that has had lasting impact on the plaintiff. Do you have any evidence that backs up your claim?"

Crany cleared his throat. "Yes, Your Honor. There is a bodycam video that the other plaintiff, Mr. Michael James, has made available to us. As you know, Mr. James was fired from his job at the Pasadena Police for refusing to destroy the video evidence."

"Objection, Your Honor!" Stacey stood up. "The video is not an official record from the Pasadena Police. An official video from the Pasadena Police does not exist."

Crany immediately intervened. "Permission to speak, Your Honor. The video was downloaded to Mr. James's own device before his superior ordered him to destroy it."

"That's a lie!" Stacey protested.

The judge pounded her gavel. "Silence! Must I remind you, Mr. Miller, that this is a preliminary hearing and all evidence is permitted. If you object to the video material, you can make a formal objection after the hearing. For now, your objection is overruled."

"Sure, Your Honor," said Stacey. Frowning, he sat down.

Crany headed to the judge's bench and handed her a piece of paper. "This is an independent evaluation of the video done by a forensics company.

The video is the original one that was on Michael's bodycam before it was ordered to be destroyed."

The judge took the paper, briefly glanced at it, and put it in her folder. "All right then. Let's see the video, Tommy."

The courtroom tech worker played the video on a laptop in the center of the room. A large screen was suspended on the left wall. The video portrayed the scene that Crany had so passionately described. It showed the kick to Tyrone's back, which caused him to instantly fall on his face and scream in pain.

The judge, who had watched the video intently, addressed Crany. "A question, Mr. Crany. Why are you using the police footage from the scene, which the defense objects to, if you could just use the shop footage?"

"Because there isn't any. The shop manager says there was a technical glitch. He showed me the video. It is unusable, ma'am."

"A glitch?" the judge asked incredulously.

"It most likely has been tampered—" Crany began.

But Stacey interrupted him. "We have the technical report that describes the issue at hand, Your Honor. Indeed, the video is unusable." He handed it to the judge, who took the document and added it to her collection of papers.

"Prosecution, you may call your first witness."

"Thank you, Your Honor. Mr. Peter McGinnis, please."

McGinnis, who had been passionately following the case, stood up. Of course, he bumped into the narrow pew when he stood up and clumsily inched out of it. At the front of the room, a courtroom tech worker stopped him before he climbed into the witness stand. McGinnis laid his hand on the Bible and swore his oath.

Crany approached him after he sat down. "Mr. McGinnis, would you mind telling us about your specific job at the Pasadena Police and how long you have been working there."

"Yes, sir. I am a homicide detective, sir. I have been in homicide for twenty-seven years. I worked ten more as a regular cop."

"Would you mind telling us what you experienced on the day of the incident? You were at headquarters, I believe...?"

Just as McGinnis was about to tell his side of the story, he noticed that Bartholdo was nervously texting on his phone. He suddenly stood up and left. *Now that's surprising*, McGinnis thought.

He said, "Yes, I was. It was a routine day for me. Just finishing up some paperwork when Michael and Fred came in. They were arguing with each other in the hallway. Then the chief, Bartholdo Meane, approached them and asked them what was going on. They told him about the scene at the store and said that Mr. Bastille had been taken away by an ambulance. The chief asked whether they'd had their bodycams on. Michael did. Mr. Meane ordered him to get rid of it. He whispered it. But you see, my office is right near where they were talking, and my door was cracked open. I usually keep it that way for ventilation. I heard everything. I know Michael. I have known him for over twenty years. He would never destroy evidence of such magnitude. He never told me that he made a copy. But what I do know is that he got fired the same week for disobeying the chief's orders. Originally, my testimony was supposed to be for Michael. To help him get his job back. I did not know...this is bigger than that." He took a clean handkerchief out of the front pocket of his tweed blazer and wiped his face. The whole ordeal had made him sweat.

"Thank you, Mr. McGinnis. That is all," Crany said.

"Does the defendant have any questions?" the judge asked.

"Yes, Your Honor." Stacey stood up and slowly walked toward the witness stand. He threw a slimy smile at McGinnis, who did not respond. "Mr. Ginnis—"

"McGinnis, sir," McGinnis said.

Stacey threw him an angry glare. "Mr. Ginnis. You said that you have known Mr. James for over twenty years. What is the nature of your relationship? Are you colleagues, friends, acquaintances? Would you mind elaborating a little bit?"

"We are friends," McGinnis said.

"Good friends?" Miller asked.

"Good friends? Yes, I guess so. Well, we are not close or anything like that."

"Is your friendship one where you have each other's backs, would you say?"

"I don't know what you mean. We all have each other's backs at the Pasadena Police."

"I would object to that. Or else Mr. James would not be sitting in this courtroom," Miller said in an admonishing tone. He threw a threatening glance at Michael, which did not escape McGinnis's notice.

"We do not cover up each other's mistakes if they are as damning as they are in Mr. Bastille's case. We tell the truth," McGinnis clarified.

"Enough!" Mr. Miller protested. "So you are good friends with Mr. James, and you have each other's backs. No further questions, Your Honor." Stacey walked away and stepped back behind his desk.

"Liars, you are!" Tyrone's grandmother shouted out of the blue.

The judge banged her gavel. "Quiet in the courtroom, or you shall be removed," she said to Mary.

Tyrone seemed to be shrinking in his wheelchair from embarrassment, McGinnis noticed as he walked back to his seat. Mrs. Bastille, however, stared the judge straight in the face, with eyes like steel.

"Any further witnesses, Mr. Crany," the judge asked him.

"Yes, Your Honor. Mr. Michael James."

"Michael James in the witness stand," the bailiff said.

Michael rose promptly, took his oath, and sat down in the witness stand.

"Mr. James, would you state your complete name and role at the Pasadena Police, please?" Crany asked.

"No problem, sir. Michael James, Sergeant at Arms, Pasadena Police."

"How long were you with the Pasadena Police before you were terminated?"

"Twenty years."

"What were your overall ratings as Sergeant at Arms, sir, if such a rating system exists at your workplace?"

"Excellent, sir. Never had any problem, sir."

"Have you ever experienced anything similar to what happened on Rosemead Boulevard?"

"Yes, sir. Many times."

"How did those go?"

"Usually without a problem, sir."

"How would you assess Mr. Bastille's behavior during the intervention? Was he overly uncooperative?"

"He was clearly distraught, sir, and verbally unruly. But nothing I haven't encountered before."

"So is it correct that he resisted Mr. Wilson's instructions at first?"

"It is true that he attempted to flee the store and that we were forced to draw our weapons. But once we had him in check, I had no further reason for concern."

"Is it correct that he refused to raise his arms?"

"Yes, at first. But he then complied. As we have seen in the video, his arms were already up when Mr. Wilson kicked him in the knee. Having him kneel down was utterly unnecessary, as you can hear me shouting in the video."

"Is it correct that Mr. Bastille lowered his left arm once he was kneeling?"

"I think he was trying to scratch himself or something. But I did not perceive it as dangerous. He was not carrying any weapons, as he repeatedly told us."

"What do you think of Mr. Wilson's decision to kick him in the back?"

"It was excessive and unnecessary, sir. The plaintiff was unarmed."

"Thank you very much, Mr. James. No further questions."

Stacey got up and approached the stand. "Mr. James. How do you know that Mr. Bastille was not carrying any weapons? Did you search him?"

"No, I did not, sir."

"So how did you know?"

"First of all, he shouted that he was unarmed at least three times. Secondly, there was no weapon visible on his waistline. The man was wearing a narrow t-shirt and jeans. I would have noticed if he was carrying something."

"But you did not pat him down?"

"No, I did not."

"Do you think it is possible that he was carrying a gun on his waistline or somewhere around his calves?"

"Of course it is possible. But highly unlikely. Especially since he told us that he was unarmed, sir, and I did not see any signs of a weapon."

"Thank you. I have no further questions, Mr. James."

"Would the prosecution like to question any more witnesses before we take a short break?" the judge asked.

"Yes, Your Honor. One more. A Mr. George Savalas has offered his testimony. I believe he is waiting outside," Crany said.

McGinnis raised an eyebrow in surprise. *Savalas? Why didn't he tell me he was coming?*

"Somebody get the witness in the stand," the judge said.

Tommy, the same guy who had played the video, walked back and exited. He came back with Savalas, who was wearing his uniform. *He's coming straight from work. I wonder if he had time for those subpoenas,* McGinnis thought as he watched Savalas take his oath.

"Mr. Savalas," Crany began, "would you mind telling the court your full name and role at the Pasadena Police."

"George Savalas, sir. Lieutenant chief's adjutant."

"Can you describe your job as a lieutenant to us a little so we can understand your role at the police?"

"Yes, sir. Well, technically, I am the chief's adjutant, sir, which means that I have a lot of executive responsibilities, such as authorizing investigations, etcetera. I am still learning, sir."

Crany was pacing back and forth again, but then he stood still. "What does that mean?"

"It means that I obtained my position a little bit too soon, sir. I have only been with the police for five years. Basically, I assist Mr. McGinnis with homicide."

"How were you able to get such a high-ranking position if you were only at the police for such a short time?"

"Special merit, sir. I busted a drug ring in downtown LA. The chief there, Orlando Lopez, recommended me when I requested a transfer."

"Why did you request a transfer?"

"I was burnt out. I wanted a lower-risk area. People died in the bust. Friends of mine."

Stacey stood up. His face was red with anger. "Objection, Your Honor. The plaintiff is moving away from the topic." He sat down.

"Objection granted," the judge said. To Crany, she said, "Come to the point, will you?"

"My apologies, Your Honor," Crany said to the judge. Then to Savalas, he said, "Anyway. You got a referral from Lopez. How does that explain how you moved up so high so quickly?"

"The new chief, sir. He needed help."

"What kind of help?"

"He doesn't read, sir."

Crany laughed and snorted at the same time. "What? The chief of the Pasadena Police cannot read?"

"I'm sorry. No. That's not what I meant. Of course Mr. Meane can read. He just doesn't read...documents."

Stacey stood up again. "Objection, Your Honor. Off topic."

However, the judge appeared interested in the discussion and did not grant the objection this time. "Have a seat, Mr. Miller. I want to hear this."

Fuming, Stacey sat down.

"What do you mean when you say he doesn't read documents? Can you elaborate a little?"

"Sure. Well, I am not saying that Mr. Meane cannot read. I have seen him walking around with a newspaper in the break room several times. However, he does seem to have difficulty reading police documents. I don't know if he doesn't understand them or if he is too busy with other things. But he would make me read his documents, and whenever his signature was needed, he would ask for my advice on whether he should sign it or not. Usually, they are permissions to open or close investigations. Just general oversight. So nothing of much consequence if handled correctly."

"So the chief assigned you his administrative tasks."

"Yes, sir."

"Would you say your chief is a competent leader?"

Stacey protested again. "Objection, Your Honor! This is completely subjective."

"Sit down, Mr. Miller," the judge said in an admonishing tone. "Let the prosecution have their turn. You will get yours."

The defense attorney snorted and sat down.

"Answer the question, Mr. Savalas," the judge said.

"Yes, Your Honor. I do not have an opinion, Your Honor."

Crany repeated incredulously, "You do not have an opinion?"

"No, sir," Savalas repeated. "It is not up to me to make that judgement."

Crany sighed.

A smile appeared on Miller's lips.

"All right then," Crany said. "Let me ask you this way. Assuming that you consider your chief a competent leader, have you encountered any situation that would lead you to think otherwise?"

Savalas looked down for a moment, then glanced at Tyrone, who was watching him intently. "I have, sir. On Sunday, when we were investigating a crime scene, he gave an interview at the scene and nearly corrupted all of the evidence."

Miller's smile vanished as quickly as it had appeared.

"I see," Crany said. "Do you have any idea why he would have chosen to do such a thing?"

"Not at all. It was very unprofessional. And I told him so."

"Do you think it is possible that he was attempting to sabotage an ongoing investigation to make our witness Mr. McGinnis, whom we just heard from, look bad?"

"It is likely that Mr. Meane is somehow involved in our current investigation, yes, sir. But we do not currently have any definitive proof."

Stacey jumped up. His chair nearly tipped over. "Speculation, Your Honor! This is outrageously out of context! We reject this witness!"

"Your Honor," Crany said, "as this is concerning an ongoing investigation that our key witness is working on, I would like Mr. Savalas's statement to go on record, as we expect more evidence to turn up. We merely want his statement to go on record so the court knows all the evidence we are considering."

"The witness's statement is permitted to go on record, Mr. Crany, but next time try to make it short, for God's sake!" the judge said, looking at his watch.

"Thank you, Your Honor," Crany said.

Both lawyers sat back down.

Crany stood back up. "No further questions, Mr. Savalas."

The judge looked at Miller. "Mr. Miller?"

"Yes, Your Honor." Stacey stood up and walked toward the witness stand. "Mr. Savalas, regarding your most recent investigation, do you have any specific proof besides Mr. Meane's television interview on Sunday?"

"As I mentioned before, due to the unclosed nature of our investigation, I cannot offer any further information," Savalas said.

"I understand, Mr. Savalas." Mr. Miller looked at the judge. "That is all, Your Honor." He walked back to his seat, where he sat down and shook his head. He threw a disparaging glance at Savalas.

"If that is all," the judge said, "you may leave the witness stand now, Mr. Savalas."

"Thank you, Your Honor," Savalas said. He stood up, climbed down from the witness stand, and headed for the door.

McGinnis attempted to make eye contact with him, but Savalas looked straight at the door.

The judge whispered something in the bailiff's ear, and the bailiff stood up and said, "The court is taking a ten-minute recess."

The judge stood up and left the courtroom.

Chapter Eighteen

McGinnis immediately stood up and rushed out. He was lucky. He found Savalas waiting for the elevator. "George! George! Wait!" He walked as quickly as he could toward the elevator.

Savalas saw him and approached him. McGinnis was breathing hard.

"Detective," Savalas said.

Looks sad, McGinnis thought. *Never seen him like this before.* "Hey, George, is everything okay with you? I had no idea you were testifying," he said.

"Considering that I will either be demoted or fired as soon as Bartholdo hears of my testimony, everything is as good as it possibly can be right now," Savalas admitted sarcastically. He was not usually the sarcastic type.

"Well, you did the right thing. What prompted you to speak out like that?"

"I called Crany as soon as you told me he had taken the case. I told him all about your suspension," Savalas said. "It was so obviously fake."

"Oh, okay. Well, thanks," McGinnis said. He took off his hat, scratched his scalp, and put it back on. "Why didn't you tell me?"

"I didn't want to impact your testimony in any way, nor your relationship with Bartholdo. I see now that I might have caused you more trouble than I could foresee. But I did it for the victim, Peter. What happened to him was not right."

"Of course. You're a good kid."

The elevator dinged.

McGinnis stopped him before he could get on. "One more thing." He pressed the elevator button for Savalas.

"Yes?"

At that moment, Bartholdo stepped out. He saw the two of them and looked straight at Savalas. "Oh, so you're here, too? Let me guess. Your testimony was not in the police's favor."

Savalas said nothing.

"Well, if that is how it is, expect consequences," Meane threatened.

McGinnis took a step toward Bartholdo. "Is that all?" he said.

Bartholdo gave McGinnis a disparaging look. "That sure is all!" he said, then walked toward the courtroom.

Both McGinnis and Savalas shrugged the encounter off.

"Anyway." McGinnis lowered his voice. "How did you get him to leave the courtroom? That was your doing, no?"

"What do you mean? I was in my office getting the request for the subpoenas ready," Savalas said. "I didn't do anything."

"What? Then why did he leave the room?"

"Maybe he had to go to the bathroom," Savalas guessed.

"No. Not for so long. But what do I know? Not important."

"Well, anyway, I still need a judge to sign those subpoenas. But the petition is in," Savalas said. "I need to go now. Not sure I can catch Wagner on another day off."

The elevator dinged again. Savalas stepped in. McGinnis saluted him with a tip of his hat and returned to the courtroom.

* * *

It was now the defense's turn to call the witnesses. The first one in the witness stand was Shilva Patel. The bailiff swore her in.

Stacey stood up, cleared his throat, and came to the witness stand. "Miss Patel, would you mind telling the court your full name and your job, please?"

"Yes, sir. My name is Shilva Patel, and I am a shop assistant at Seven Eleven on Rosemead Boulevard."

"Are you the person who called the police on July fifteenth, the day when Mr. Tyrone Bastille was arrested at your shop?"

"Yes, sir. I was the one who called."

"Very well, Miss Patel. Would you mind telling us what prompted you to call the police? Feel free to take as much time as you need to describe your situation."

"It is like we have seen in the video, only the problem started before. Like other witnesses have said, Mr. Tyrone was causing problems. Apparently, I served a customer who had cut in front of him in line. I did not notice this." Shilva looked Tyrone straight in the eye. "Mr. Tyrone, I am very sorry about that."

She turned back toward Miller. "Mr. Tyrone first shouted at the customer in front of him, who just paid and ignored him. Then Mr. Tyrone followed him to the door, but the customer closed the door in his face. I think the door must have hit his face, so he started cursing and shouting really loud. Then he came at me and started insulting me. He would not stop shouting. When I asked him to leave the shop, he refused. I asked him three times to leave. I told him that I have the right to deny service to customers who are acting unsafe. So he called me a racist slut."

Shilva looked at the judge. "Your Honor, I was not being a racist by refusing service to Tyrone. I was just feeling unsafe. So I called the police. And I am very sorry for what happened to Tyrone. The rest, you saw for yourself in the video."

Stacey had been pacing up and down the front of the courtroom. He appeared tense. He finally stood still. "Miss Patel, how were you feeling when Tyrone was shouting at you in front of other customers?"

"I felt annoyed, sir, and unsafe."

"Were you afraid?"

"Yes, sir, very."

"Why were you so afraid? Were you worried he was going to draw a weapon?"

"Yes, Mr. Miller. I was afraid he might attack me and other customers in the store, sir. That's why I refused to serve him."

"Could you tell from looking at him whether he carried a weapon?"

"No, I could not."

"How afraid were you, Miss Patel? Were you afraid for your life, or was it not so bad?"

"I have never been in such a situation before, sir. I was not only afraid for my life but also for the lives of the other customers. There was a woman with a child in there, sir."

"Thank you so much for sharing your side of the story with us, Miss Patel. No further questions." Stacey contently strode back to his seat.

"Does the prosecution have any questions for this witness?"

Crany stood up. "Yes, Your Honor, I do." He walked to the witness stand. "Miss Patel, what were you thinking when the police began handling Mr. Bastille. Did you think he was being treated correctly? Fairly?"

Shilva glanced nervously between Crany and Miller. A long moment of silence began.

"Answer the question," the judge ordered.

"At first, I was just glad that they came so quickly. But then, when they drew their weapons, I got scared and lay down. Whatever followed, I only heard from behind the counter. I did not see it. I was lying down."

"Important detail, Miss Patel. Thank you for mentioning that. Did you hear Mr. James give Fred Wilson any specific instructions?"

"Yes, sir. I heard somebody say, 'Stop it! He is unarmed,' and other similar things. But I was still scared."

"Of course you were, Miss Patel. One more question. Does the video we saw earlier portray the reality you experienced?"

"Yes, sir, from what I can tell, it is real."

"Objections, Your Honor!"

"Go ahead, Mr. Miller."

"Miss Patel would not be able to verify the material if she was lying down behind the counter."

"Granted," the judge said.

"No further questions. Thank you, Miss Patel." Crany walked back and sat down next to Tyrone. Crany gave him a gentle pat on the back.

"You may leave the witness stand, Miss Patel," the judge said.

Shilva left the witness stand and rushed out of the courtroom.

Looks like she's had enough, McGinnis thought.

He watched as Bartholdo was called to the stand and sworn in. *Let's see what the old chief has to say about this now.*

152

"Mr. Meane, please state your full name and role at the Pasadena Police," Miller asked Meane.

"Bartholdo Meane, chief of police, Pasadena."

"How long have you held this position, if I may ask?"

"Three years. Going on four," Bartholdo said.

"Would you consider yourself efficient at your position, or do you feel that you are still learning?"

"Still learning, sir," Bartholdo said.

"What do you mean by that? Can you give the court an example?"

"The situation at the scene on Sunday, sir. I can see now that giving an interview on site was a mistake," he said, glancing at the judge.

"How come, sir? Can you explain?"

"I was badgered by a team of reporters that had been called by some onlookers. The body was in plain sight on a highly frequented hiking trail in Pasadena, sir. Eaton Canyon. When the journalists tried to access the crime scene, I stepped in front of the site to block access and started answering questions while I ordered Mr. Savalas to put up a screen that prevented people from seeing the body. Apparently, that was a mistake, sir."

"That sounds like a fairly good explanation, sir. Brings up a question. Where was the homicide detective who should have been investigating?"

"Mr. McGinnis was not there yet. Mr. Savalas, my adjutant lieutenant, was attempting to reach him, to no avail."

"Ah, I see. The homicide detective who should have been overseeing the site was not doing his job," Mr. Miller said.

"Objection, Your Honor!" Crany jumped up. "That is an interpretation."

"Sustained," the judge said, and continued to listen.

Frustrated, Crany sat back down.

"Since we are talking about the homicide detective, let's talk about the scene in the hallway that he described. Do you recall any such scene, Mr. Meane?"

"No, sir. That story is made up. Mr. Wilson and Mr. James came straight to my office."

"So you did not discuss the events at the Seven Eleven shop in the hallway at all?"

"Never. Anything that was ever said was discussed in my office. The homicide detective is lying."

"No further questions. Thank you, Mr. Meane," Stacey said before walking away.

Crany stood up and approached the stand. "Mr. Meane, on what day did the scene at Eaton Canyon occur?"

"It happened on a Sunday, sir."

"Was Mr. McGinnis on active duty that day?"

"Not on active duty, but he was supposed to be on call."

"And what happened eventually? Did Mr. McGinnis ever show up?"

"Yes, he did. After many attempts at calling him. And I believe Mr. Savalas had to go and pick him up."

Crany raised an eyebrow in surprise. "Oh? Why?"

"I think Mr. McGinnis's car broke down or something," Bartholdo said, laughing at him. "The man drives a nineteen seventy-five Ford Futura or some absurd vehicle like that. Totally unreliable."

Crany cringed. "At what time did Mr. McGinnis ultimately arrive at the scene, then?"

"He arrived around eight thirty, I would say" Bartholdo said.

"And at what time did Mr. Savalas first call him?"

"I am not sure," Bartholdo muttered. "Maybe at seven or seven thirty?"

"So Mr. McGinnis made it in one or one and a half hours to a crime scene on a Sunday morning when he was off duty, his car broke down, and his colleague had to come and pick him up?"

"Yeah, he did." Bartholdo snorted and shook his head. "Man needs a new car."

"Well, I don't see how you are calling this man unreliable when he did everything in his power to show up at a scene when his car was not functioning. On the contrary." Crany stepped away from the witness stand and focused on the judge. "I would not only call that very reliable but extremely committed. No further questions." He returned to his seat.

Chapter Nineteen

The court hearing had lasted well into the early afternoon. The multiple attempts to destroy his and Savalas's characters had left McGinnis emotionally depleted. He was well aware of the detrimental consequences his habit of handling emotional distress by excessively consuming food had on his waistline, but he decided to seek out the nearest burger joint rather than face the chief in person. Too ashamed to ask the fit Savalas to come along, McGinnis went there alone and ate as much as his heart desired.

Eventually, he headed back to headquarters. Traffic was quiet for a Wednesday afternoon, and the heat seemed to have subsided slightly. When he got there, he took a deep breath before entering through the automated steel door. He immediately went into the administrative part of the police building. He carefully took one step at a time as he went up to the second floor, hoping that he would not run into Bartholdo.

"Oh, and here comes the liar." Bartholdo greeted him at the top of the stairs. Savalas was standing right next to him.

"I said what I heard, and if you don't like what I said, that is your problem, not mine," McGinnis defended himself.

"We shall see whose problem it is. But for now, I am leaving it at Mr. Savalas's demotion. He is to be considered second lieutenant. The adjunct position has been awarded to Mr. Fred Wilson on an interim basis," Bartholdo said.

Fred was grinning at them from inside Meane's office. McGinnis and Savalas exchanged a glance and openly shook their heads.

"That is it, Mr. Savalas. If you would like to reconsider your position, see me in my office."

"No, sir," Savalas said.

"I see what you're doing here, Chief," McGinnis spoke up. "You tried to pull something similar with me. But let me give you a word of advice. Keep treating an organization full of good, competent policemen like they are idiots, and you are the one who will hang, not me or Savalas here."

"That's nonsense!" Bartholdo shouted. He stomped off into his office and slammed the door.

Officer Smith came around the corner. "Woah-ho, what was that all about? Never seen the chief so angry."

"He doesn't like it when people tell the truth about him. Makes him look bad in public," McGinnis said.

"I bet," Officer Smith said. He snickered and walked off.

McGinnis studied Savalas, who looked pale and haggard. *Sad dog*, McGinnis thought. "You haven't had anything to eat yet, have you?" he asked him.

"No, I haven't."

"That's what I thought," McGinnis said, then showed him the lunch bag he had saved from the burger joint. "Saved you the fries. I can't eat that stuff anymore if I want to live to be sixty." He handed him the box full of half-warm French fries.

"Oh, thanks!" Savalas said. He took the box.

"Your office or my office?" McGinnis asked.

"Your office," Savalas said, then followed him down the corridor.

By the time they reached McGinnis's office, the fries were gone. Savalas threw the empty box into the recycling bin and sat down in an old-school chair. McGinnis hung his hat on the rack behind his door and walked around the desk to sit down.

"Boy, what a day!" McGinnis sighed.

"You can say that out loud," Savalas agreed.

"The man was flat-out lying under oath," McGinnis said. He pointed at his office door, which they had closed behind them. "That conversation took place right in front of this door."

"I know," Savalas said. "I heard it, too."

"What? You knew about it and never said anything to me?"

"It's not like you told me what you were going to be saying under oath. It all just came out at the hearing today."

"Gosh, you need to tell Bob Crany about this. I mean, they are going to need someone to back up my claim."

"Oh, no worries. I'm sure there will be a chance to do that. But if you ask me, that video is proof enough. I mean hell, he kicked that guy twice for no reason!"

"You think they are going to approve it?"

"Hell yes! There is no doubt that was Michael's footage. Bartholdo can say what he wants. You think they messed with the shop video, too?"

"I would not be surprised if they did. Crany should have that investigated. Anyway, we're getting off topic. We need to strategize."

"I don't have the subpoenas yet. We are going to have to figure out something else," Savalas said. "Wagner did not get back to me."

At that moment, McGinnis's phone rang, and he answered it, spitting out, "Detective!" Then he said, "I said don't call me that. Who? What? Seriously? Today? Okay, come and show it to me. At the coffee shop. Yes. That one. When? Right now! Give me thirty minutes." He hung up, stood up, and walked to the rack behind his door, where he grabbed his hat.

"What was that all about?" Savalas asked. He turned on the old-school chair to watch McGinnis's movements.

"That was Bartholdo's old classmate. He has something," McGinnis said.

"Who's that?" Savalas asked.

"Zeke, the guy who's repairing my car. He gave me the yearbook"

"For real? Didn't he drive the tow truck, too?"

McGinnis nodded.

"That's screwed up!" Savalas protested, then shrugged.

"Well, he got me the information!" McGinnis defended his method.

"You going there alone?" Savalas asked.

"I am."

"Sure you don't need backup?"

"Positive. Zeke's a bit off the rocker, but he's on our side."

"All right then." Savalas sighed and stood up. "I shall work on those subpoenas, then."

McGinnis carefully placed his hat on his delicate head. "Oh shoot. I'm gonna need a ride. You mind?"

"Not at all," Savalas said, grabbing his keys.

"Let's use the squad car," McGinnis said.

Astounded, Savalas stood still. "Why?"

"Intuition."

* * *

Savalas stopped in front of Nell's Café. The playground nearby was buzzing, with children playing on their scooters, bikes, and the play structures, enjoying the cooler evening air. McGinnis slid out as elegantly as he could without pulling himself up by holding the doorframe.

"Sure you don't want me to come?" Savalas asked.

McGinnis turned around and leaned on the open doorframe. "No. You're in uniform. I don't wanna attract any attention. Especially since Zeke's not an official member of our team."

"Gotcha. Well then, till later."

"Yeah. I'll keep you posted."

"Wait a minute. Aren't you gonna need a ride back to headquarters?"

"I don't know. Maybe Nell will lend me her car."

"How about this. I'll pull over farther down here on South Michigan and wait there for you."

"Sure. If you don't mind sweating in the hot car?"

"No worries. I can handle it. It's starting to cool down, anyway."

"All right then. Till later." McGinnis let go of the doorframe and closed it.

At that moment, he saw Zeke slipping into the café as if he were trying to sneak past them. McGinnis gave him time to enter and let Savalas pull out of sight.

McGinnis walked over and entered the café. Of course, Zeke was standing at the counter ordering something. Nell, who was preparing a salad on the back counter, saw the detective enter, but he winked and motioned with his hand for her to be silent. She smiled and looked down at the salad, which appeared to be finished.

McGinnis approached Zeke and nudged him. "Hey there, Zeke. You trying to avoid me or something?"

Zeke, who had just paid, looked at him and then whispered, "No, boss. Just trying not to reveal myself in front of the entire public as your official informant." McGinnis grimaced.

"Large tropical iced tea," a girl behind the counter said.

"That's mine!" Zeke said, grabbing it.

Nell, who had been watching the scene from the back, whispered something into the girl's ear. The girl grabbed another cup, filled it with the same drink, and offered it to McGinnis. "Iced tea?"

"Sure, thank you!"

Nell winked at him as he grabbed it.

"All right, where do you want to talk?" Zeke asked. "It's a bit crowded here."

"That's exactly what I was hoping for. No one will notice anything. That table over there will do." McGinnis pointed at the last table along the wall.

Zeke and McGinnis sat down. McGinnis worked very hard not to knock down Zeke's drink as he sat down. The table was a little bit wobbly.

"All right. What have you got for me?" McGinnis whispered. The café was quite noisy, which made his voice disappear in the rest of the rumble.

"You told me to film it when your suspect met with any...familiar people?"

"Yes, why? Did she?"

"Take a look for yourself. This was behind the courthouse on Thurgood Marshall Street earlier today. I figured you were stuck at the hearing, so I didn't call you until after lunch."

"You could have texted me—'"

"No, no. Look at this!" Zeke gave him his phone and pressed play.

McGinnis noticed that the camera was focused on a Fiat 500e. It was parked on Thurgood Marshall Street, and Marisella, dressed in a flashy red dress, stepped out carrying a small handbag that she pressed tightly to her body. While she went to the meter to put money in it, the video suddenly shifted focus. Barthold Meane, dressed in full police gear—the same outfit he had been wearing at the court hearing—came rushing down Euclid Avenue and headed straight toward Marisella, who waited for him next to the parking meter.

Bartholdo addressed her aggressively. "What do you want?"

"The rest of the money. It was supposed to be fifty thousand."

"I already told you before that you are not getting any more. You screwed up. Screwed up big time. I am risking my career cleaning up after you. So you take what you got and get lost."

"I'm not going anywhere, Bartholdo. I already thought of running away. But I did not risk everything to walk away empty-handed. You are going to give me the rest, or—"

Bartholdo laughed in her face. "Or what? You going to talk?" Again, he laughed. "No, you're not! Because if you talk, you know where you are going. Back to prison!" He laughed even louder. "I'm really sorry, sweetie. But you're going to have to figure this out yourself. I am done with you."

"The money!" McGinnis could hear that Marisella's voice was quivering. She took a gun out of her small handbag and aimed it at Bartholdo.

"I wouldn't do that, sweetie. This is the civic center. There are cameras everywhere. I have a court hearing to go back to!"

Confidently, Bartholdo turned around and abruptly walked away. Taking huge steps, he walked rapidly back up Euclid Avenue. Marisella lowered her unfired weapon and watched him walk away. Bartholdo did not turn around once. Then the camera zoomed in on Marisella's face. She was still standing there next to the meter, her Browning Buckmark pointing at nothing as she cried. She eventually lowered her weapon and climbed back into her car.

McGinnis held on to Zeke's phone. "You know you're going to have to leave that with me."

"But my contacts! How am I going to be able to do my job if nobody can call me?"

"You have my car. I have your phone. We're even!"

Zeke gaped at McGinnis. "No 'thank you, great job,' or 'oh my God, that's an amazing piece of evidence, and that's exactly what I was looking for'?"

"One thing at a time. First, we're going to catch this lady, and then we will see. I would also like my car back at some point."

"It's ready, boss! All I am waiting for is the paint that I ordered."

McGinnis stood up. He knocked over Zeke's iced tea and raised his voice. "How many times have I told you not to call me that?"

Zeke somehow managed to catch his cup before too much of his drink spilled.

McGinnis handed him a napkin so he could take care of the rest. "Sorry. Here. Use this."

"Yes, boss. Thank you, boss!" Zeke said, wiping off the table.

McGinnis left the café, cringing. An unexpected gust of wind nearly knocked off his hat. He knew that if he turned around, he would see Nell's smiling face through the window. He took off his hat and slipped it into his blazer pocket. He lifted his gaze up to the sky, where rainclouds were beginning to form. He walked to Savalas's squad car, which was on South Michigan, one block south of Nell's Café. The windows were down.

McGinnis knocked on the windshield. "Hey there. I think it's going to rain."

McGinnis's arrival woke Savalas, who had dozed off. "Wait, what? Rain? In September?"

"Yeah, looks like a thunderstorm is about to come. See for yourself!"

Savalas, who was still in the process of coming back to the present, stuck his head out the window and looked up. "Clouds! For real! Woah, we can sure use some rain."

McGinnis let himself into the passenger side, and Savalas pulled his upper torso back into the car.

"Anything useful?" Savalas asked. Sweat was dripping from his forehead despite the wind.

"Jackpot! Bartholdo paid Marisella off, just like we thought. Question is, for how many bodies? Here. Watch!" He showed Savalas the video on Zeke's phone.

The lieutenant's jaw dropped. "My God! We need to get Bartholdo away from the Pasadena Police immediately!"

"Not so quick, pal. First, we are going to pay our friend Marisella Wawrinski another visit."

"Right now?" A reluctant frown snuck across Savalas's exhausted forehead.

McGinnis strapped himself in. "Right now!"

Chapter Twenty

For the third time in one week, Savalas and McGinnis headed to 1097 East Orange Grove . By the time they got there, the wind was already knocking down palm fronds from the tall trees. A flood warning came in on both the detective's and the lieutenant's cell phones.

"Looks like we're headed for a big storm!" Savalas said.

They pulled up to the curb at 1097 East and watched Marisella place a suitcase into the trunk of her electric Fiat. She was wearing the same red dress they had seen in the video. The stunning red garment was flapping erratically against her skinny figure. A brown curl came loose from her neatly tied bun. The Fiat was plugged in to charge.

"What's she all dressed up for, anyway? She going to a ball or something?" Savalas asked.

"Goin' out of town, I'd say. Some like to make it fancy," McGinnis said.

Marisella finally saw them. Immediately, she dashed around the small car, ripped the cable out, and jumped in.

"Wait! I'll get out and stop her. She won't run me over." McGinnis struggled with the seatbelt. By the time he got it off, Marisella was already speeding down Orange Grove.

"Aw, shutterbusters!" McGinnis cursed. "I can't get this thing off."

"Looks like we're going to have to resort to Plan B!" Savalas said, stepping on the gas. The Fiat in front of them was moving like a rocket-ship. "Darn it! That little car is fast!"

"It's because it's electric. They have much simpler combustion engines. They don't need to shift gears to get from zero to full speed," McGinnis said. He held on to the doorframe as Savalas moved in and out of the right lane frequently.

While attempting to overtake the car, Savalas nearly hit an SUV that was coming from the other direction. There was a huge crack of thunder, a torrential downpour started.

"Watch it, man!" McGinnis shouted.

"No worries. I got this," Savalas said, steering clear of a truck that was headed his way.

The traffic light on Lake Street had just turned yellow when Marisella flew under it. Savalas turned on his siren and crossed Lake Street on a red light. He barely missed a car that was attempting to make a left turn.

"Darn it!" Savalas cursed. "We're losing her!"

"Chances are that if she was charging her car, she's going to run out of power. Those Fiats don't go far."

"Let me get some reinforcements." Savalas turned on the broadband and grabbed the handheld microphone. "This is unit thirteen. Lieutenant George Savalas. We have a suspect in a gray Fiat speeding down Orange Grove in the direction of Rose Bowl. We need reinforcements so we can apprehend."

"Roger that. Unit twenty-four officers Smith and Gonzalez are on Fair Oaks. Where should I send them?"

"Have them wait for us at Orange Grove. If they see the Fiat, follow it!" Savalas said, then dumped the microphone back in its holder.

The street was quiet for a while. All McGinnis could hear was the rain pounding on the car roof.

"There she is!" She was stuck at a red light on Fair Oaks. "And there's Gonzalez and Smith right behind her!" McGinnis shouted.

Savalas was merely half a block behind. "Aw! She's turning right on Lincoln," he said.

"I have a feeling she's heading toward the Rose Bowl," McGinnis said.

"Why would she go there?"

"I have no idea, but I don't think she's going to be going much farther. Although there is a chance she might try to get away on the freeway. If she does that, we will have the entire freeway brigade follow her until her power runs out. But let's wait and see what she does next," McGinnis said calmly.

Savalas turned right on Lincoln and was only two cars behind the Fiat. Sure enough, she passed under the 210, then turned left on Seco Street.

"See that? Headed straight for the Rose Bowl," McGinnis said confidently.

Savalas shook his head in confusion, then hit the brakes abruptly. A runner crossed right in front of him. The squad car sat still. The runner, who was soaking wet, did a double take. The track around the Rose Bowl was entirely deserted aside from him.

"Be careful, man!" Savalas shouted, sounding distressed.

Unlike him, McGinnis was enjoying the ride. "Look! She's getting on Arroyo Boulevard."

Savalas caught up and was now right behind Unit 24, which was right behind the Fiat. A lonesome dog walker wearing purple rain gear that matched his gray Schnauzer's jacket was walking along the dirt path that paralleled Arroyo Boulevard and the concrete channel of the Arroyo River. He turned his head when he saw the three cars going way above the speed limit. The parking lot to the left was empty.

The Fiat passed underneath the Holly Street walking bridge. Its dark, water-drenched concrete arches loomed threateningly in the torrential rain. Unit 24 and Savalas followed as the Fiat climbed up the steep hill, nearing the Colorado Bridge. The four massive arches of the Arroyo Seco Bridge were entwined in a wild jungle of ancient Oak treetops that swayed in the wind. Broken leaves and branches fell into the Arroyo Park below.

A heavy gust of wind nearly threw Savalas off track. "Wow!" he said, straightening the steering wheel.

McGinnis, who had never let go of the handle on the doorframe, did not flinch. "Correct me if I'm wrong," he said. "But can it be that she is slowing down?"

Sure enough, before any of the cops were aware of what was going on, Marisella abruptly stopped and jumped out of her vehicle at the Arroyo Seco

Trail entry. She disappeared nearly instantly under the cover of trees on the trail.

"Shutterbusters!" McGinnis cursed and unstrapped himself. He was not looking forward to getting drenched in the rain. He put his hat back on his head and stepped out.

Unit 24 had already pulled up at the curb. Officer Smith had attempted to stop her already, but Marisella was faster. Smith and Gonzalez waited for orders from Savalas.

"What do we do?" Smith asked.

"George, you go after her and see if you can catch her before she does something stupid. You two stay here and secure the vehicle. I am going with Savalas."

McGinnis pulled the collar of his tweed blazer up, buttoned every button he could find, and marched forward onto the trail. He had to use his hands to catch wet twigs that were whipping into his face. He did his best to keep up with Savalas but stopped every couple of minutes to catch his breath. The rain eventually subsided and gave way to an even heavier wind. McGinnis briefly looked up at the sky. *Aw, sky's gonna open up again soon. We coulda used some more of this rain.*

The windy trail led him along the shallow Arroyo Seco river and under the dark-gray concrete arches of the freeway bridge, where he was momentarily protected from the whipping winds and wet branches. As soon as he stepped out from under the arches, though, another downpour drenched him from the inside out. *Didn't meant that so literally,* he thought to himself as he glanced again at the sky.

The trail continued along the smelly stream of the Arroyo Seco. He was now facing the gloomy arches of the Colorado Bridge, which led across the Arroyo rivulet.

Savalas ripped him out of his weather-related thoughts. "Detective! I have her. She's here!"

McGinnis slowly jogged so he could catch up with Savalas, who was protected from the rain under the Colorado Bridge. McGinnis watched as Marisella jumped from the crown of a young oak tree and landed on the rim of the bridge's foundation. She carefully balanced herself and made her way toward the first arch, where she balanced on her hands and feet in an attempt to climb up. Her bun had fallen apart, and her dress stuck tightly to her thin body. Her ballerina shoe came off and nearly fell on McGinnis's head. Savalas caught it and held onto it.

"Goddamn it!" McGinnis shouted. "Come off that bridge, Marisella! You are going to kill yourself! We know what happened. Let us help you!"

But Marisella did not listen. She continued to climb up the slippery arch, holding on with her hands and feet. *How on earth is she not slipping off?* McGinnis wondered.

Savalas and McGinnis studied the surroundings.

"We can get her off, Savalas, but we are going to need a fire truck."

Savalas immediately grabbed his walkie-talkie. "This is George Savalas, Pasadena Police. We need a fire truck for a suicide rescue. Yes, with a ladder. Underneath the Colorado Bridge. Yes, the east end. There is service access underneath the bridge."

McGinnis walked to the service gate under the bridge. "Damn it! It's locked! Savalas! Tell dispatch to contact public works for access!"

"We need access from public works. Yes, public works. Tell them it's an emergency operation. Suicide!" Savalas put the walkie-talkie back on his belt and stepped out from under the bridge.

Marisella was now at a height where a fall would either kill her immediately or the trees underneath the bridge would shred her skin to pieces if she landed on them.

"Geez! How did she even get up there so high without slipping?" Savalas said.

McGinnis came out from under the bridge. A gust of wind nearly blew his hat off, but he caught it on time. Marisella made an attempt at standing up, but the wind nearly blew her off. She went back down on her hands and knees.

"Marisella!" McGinnis tried again. "We know that Bartholdo Meane is behind this. We have it on video. Your last encounter behind the courthouse! We filmed it!"

"Leave me alone!" Marisella shouted. "I'm not going back to jail. I don't want to live anymore. Go away!" Her body kept slipping down the wet arch, but she somehow managed to pull herself up. Again, she tried standing up. Her red dress was flapping in the wind.

McGinnis heard the sirens of the fire engine approaching, and Marisella looked up, most likely able to see the truck from her position up there.

"I told you to leave me alone!" she shouted.

"Marisella, we are not going anywhere. Neither is the fire truck. We know that Bartholdo paid you off. We need your testimony! If you tell us what happened, then we can make a plea deal with you. Nobody can change what you did, but if you agree to cooperate, we can arrange for you to have all the support you need to make it through this. I know you wanted to talk. You planted the proof when you broke into my apartment! We will help you. But we need your testimony to prove that Bartholdo was behind all of it."

The fire truck parked at the entrance of the locked gate. One of the fire fighters stepped out and rattled it. "How do we get through?"

"We called public works. They should be here shortly. I recommend you take a look from that side," Savalas said, pointing at McGinnis.

The fireman stalked around the concrete pillar and passed a jungle of wet leaves, heading toward McGinnis. "Oh dear. How did she even get up there?" he asked when he was standing beside him.

"I have no idea. Must have rubber on her feet or something."

"I don't know if I could do that," the firefighter, who was as tall and strong as Savalas, admitted.

"Can you get her off there?" McGinnis asked.

"Once we get past the gate, no problem. We can use the service road to get the truck closer and then get her off there with the ladder."

"Great!" McGinnis said.

Finally, McGinnis saw a City of Pasadena vehicle approach and park behind the fire engine. A tiny man stepped out. Keys were dangling from his left hand. "Who is in charge here?" he asked.

Savalas showed his badge. "Lieutenant Savalas, Pasadena Police. We have a suicide rescue."

"Suicide? I thought we were done with suicides when we installed the barriers."

"She is not on the bridge, sir. She is under it. We need you to unlock this gate immediately and give access to this fire truck."

"Yes, sir," the small man said, grabbing the key. He opened the gate without further questions.

The fireman who had been talking to McGinnis went back to his truck. He jumped in on the driver's side, started the motor, and slowly drove past the gate to the concrete service road. He stopped the engine underneath the highest point of the first arch. Then the ladder was released and rotated northward. A second fireman climbed along the closed ladder toward the extension platform at the end.

"Ready!" he shouted.

McGinnis continued talking to Marisella. "All right, they are coming to get you now. You don't need to be afraid. They have a lot of experience with these things."

"Stop them, or I am going to jump!" Marisella threatened.

"Stop!" McGinnis said to the firemen. He made a motion with his hand for them to stop the operation.

The ladder stopped extending.

"Marisella! Let us help you!"

Marisella, who had made another attempt at standing up, finally crouched down and held on to the concrete. McGinnis could see from his position on the ground that she was shivering. He couldn't tell for sure, but it appeared to him that she was crying.

"Okay, I give up," he heard her whimpering.

McGinnis gave the driver in the engine a thumbs-up. The ladder continued to extend until the man at the end reached where Marisella was sitting crouched on the arch. He opened the barrier on the extension platform and gave Marisella his hand. She held on to it immediately and jumped onto the platform and into safety.

McGinnis let out a huge sigh of relief and put his hat back on. Savalas looked at him for an update. McGinnis gave him a thumbs-up and began to clap. Savalas walked over to McGinnis, who was still standing in the middle of the walking trail, and joined in on the clapping. At once, all the firemen and the tiny little man from public works applauded as they watched the ladder be lowered until Marisella and the fireman were safely on the ground.

Chapter Twenty-One

The mental health professional, a black woman in her forties, had arrived at the scene. She was about to go to Marisella, but Savalas stopped her and said, "You cannot be here. She is a suspect in a homicide investigation."

"Audrey Simpson. I'm from suicide prevention. They called me because somebody—that young woman over there, I gather—was attempting to jump. It is my job to consult her."

"Yes, ma'am," Savalas said. "I understand that. However, we are in the midst of our investigation and need to speak with her first."

McGinnis showed her his license. "Peter McGinnis, homicide detective. You are from suicide prevention, I gather?"

"Yes, Mr. McGinnis. Audrey Simpson. I am here to speak with that young woman over there."

McGinnis and Audrey shook hands.

"I have a suggestion to make, Ms. Simpson. Seeing that Miss Wawrinski is a key witness in an ongoing homicide investigation, we are going to need to take her into custody and interrogate her immediately." McGinnis watched as Audrey's forehead began to wrinkle. "However, this is what I would suggest. Considering the obvious emotional distress that our witness is under, we would welcome it if you could offer her your support after our conversation with her."

Audrey pondered over it. "Where is she going to be held in custody? In Pasadena?"

McGinnis glanced at Savalas. "Actually, no. Since she is connected to a case that occurred outside of our jurisdiction, we have to bring her to the County Department on Temple Street."

Savalas raised an eyebrow.

"Why downtown?" Audrey asked, confused.

"Her case is connected with the LA County Department administration," McGinnis explained.

The firefighter brought Marisella to Audrey. "I believe Ms. Simpson is going to take over from here," he said, clearly having no idea that Marisella was a homicide suspect.

Savalas casually gave Marisella her shoe back, which she slipped onto her mud-drenched foot.

Audrey pulled out a blanket that she had stuffed into her handbag and put it around Marisella's shoulders. "Here. That should keep you warm. I'm Audrey Simpson from suicide prevention. What's your name?"

Marisella looked at her with big eyes. "Marisella...Wawrinski." Mascara was running down her wet cheeks from the tears that she had cried. Her hair was all undone.

"Here!" McGinnis offered her his handkerchief and made a motion for her to clean up her face.

Marisella wiped off the rainwater, smearing the makeup even more. She gave him back the mascara-stained handkerchief without a word.

"But I understand that Mr. McGinnis needs to speak with you first."

"Ms. Simpson, meet us at the downtown LASD headquarters within the hour. Ask for Detective Orlando Lopez. We are taking Miss Wawrinski into custody now."

McGinnis grabbed Marisella by the arm and began hiking back with her on the wet trail. Savalas immediately followed behind them.

Marisella gaped at McGinnis, terrified. "But...Bartholdo... He is going—"

"Don't worry, Marisella. We are not taking you to Pasadena. You are going to be staying at the police facility downtown. Mr. Meane will not be able to bother you there."

Marisella gazed around helplessly as she was forced to hike on the muddy trail.

"Lieutenant!"

"Yes, Detective!" Savalas answered very formally.

"Call your old boss, Mr. Lopez, and tell him that we are bringing him a suspect in the Alfio Cordini case."

"Sure, Detective. Consider it done," Savalas said, dialing at once.

"And we are taking her in your private car if you don't mind," McGinnis added.

"You want me to drive to headquarters and change cars? Why?" Savalas asked. His eyebrows were squeezed together in confusion.

"Just a precaution. You will see," McGinnis said.

Marisella's forehead wrinkled with grief and horror.

* * *

McGinnis, Savalas, and Marisella arrived in the lobby of 211 West Temple Street merely forty-five minutes after the incident on the bridge. The receptionist called Lopez.

A few minutes later, the elevator dinged, and Lopez stepped out. "You guys from the Pasadena PD just can't get enough of me, can you? What on earth happened to you all?"

It was only then that McGinnis became aware of how they were all drenched to the bone. A small puddle was beginning to form under his feet because of his dripping clothes.

For once, Lopez's breath was not reeking, McGinnis noticed with relief.

"What have we here?" Lopez said, studying Marisella, whose mascara was smeared all over her face. She was wearing handcuffs.

"It's best you hear her out yourself. But before we can do that, we need to request an interrogation room."

"Why not in Pasadena?"

"Which version of the answer do you want? The official one or the real one?"

Lopez looked utterly confused. "I don't know. Is there a difference?"

"Let me just put it this way. This woman here can tell you exactly how Alfio Cordini died and how much the whole operation cost," McGinnis said.

Marisella did not respond. She kept her gaze steady on a point on the marble floor.

"But I thought we said that you were investigating the case now?"

"We are going to need to bring the case back to the original area of jurisdiction. At least until an official investigation at the Pasadena PD has been launched. I'm afraid that if we keep Marisella in Pasadena, she will not be safe. And she is the crucial witness in both investigations. Alfio Cordini's and Helen Johnson's. You may also want to take a look at this before we begin the official interrogation." McGinnis gave Lopez Zeke's phone and showed him the video of Bartholdo's encounter with Marisella behind the courthouse.

"Holy moly, are you telling me that *he* is behind all this?"

"I don't know. I think Marisella here knows more about it than I currently do," McGinnis said.

"Wait. Wait a minute. You mean you want me to hold Marisella here because...because she's not safe up there because of...Bartholdo?"

Both McGinnis and Savalas nodded.

"Holy crap! That's...bad!"

McGinnis and Savalas nodded in agreement.

"Let me get you guys something dry to wear first." Lopez said to the receptionist, "Hey, you. Can you get these people some dry clothes?"

The receptionist sized them up. "Uh..."

"Great, thank you! Have them brought upstairs to my office." To the other three, Lopez said, "All right, let's get into a room where we can talk." He pressed the elevator button behind him.

The elevator arrived, and they all stepped in.

* * *

"All right, Miss Wawrinski. You have a seat here," Lopez said, guiding her to a seat at the long table. "You guys can find your own seats."

Lopez sat down at the end of the table, right next to Marisella. McGinnis whispered something in Savalas's ear. Savalas left the room quietly. McGinnis eventually lowered himself into the chair opposite Marisella.

"All right, Marisella, if you want us to keep you safe, you are going to have to tell your whole story, and you are going to have to tell it to Mr. Lopez here. He's the homicide detective who was originally in charge of Alfio Cordini's murder. He is a big deal down here and can keep Bartholdo away from you. But only if you tell him why."

McGinnis sighed audibly, took off his drenched hat, and wrung it out on the floor. Lopez gave him the stink eye.

"Sorry! It was dripping all over my face."

Lopez jumped up, picked up the phone, and spoke to the people outside the room. "Where are those darn clothes? What? You can't find any? We are a police department. We have uniforms and jail clothes! Yes, get them. What size? You saw for yourself, didn't you?" He hung the phone up and sat back down. "You have to do everything yourself in this house."

McGinnis snickered slightly, then focused back on Marisella. She was sitting there staring at the same spot she'd been staring at when she sat down.

"Marisella?"

She finally raised her gaze. "What about that lady at the bridge? Audrey, I think she said was her name. You said I could talk to her."

"Yes, we will get you all the mental health support that you want, along with a lawyer to make a good case for you. But not until you have told me and Lopez what happened. Every little tidbit."

"All right," Marisella said. She looked McGinnis straight in the eye. "Helen was my roommate. My first and only friend. I was jealous of Alfio because they were expecting a baby together, but not jealous enough to kill him! That was not my idea. Never!" Frustrated, she put both her elbows on the table and held her face.

"All right. This is how it all began." She let go of her face, took a deep breath, and sat up. "When they released me from Linwood Regional Detention Center five years ago, they allowed me to call my old lawyer, Leslie Meyers."

"Leslie Meyers, the family lawyer from Sierra Madre?"

"Yes, her. The one who is married to that Persian guy. Andrew something. The one that Helen had a crush on."

McGinnis and Lopez exchanged a glance.

Marisella went on. "She defended me in my murder trial. The guy who I sat in Linwood for raped me. But I was never able to prove it, so they gave me twenty years. Almost the full sentence for murder. I don't think Leslie ever took another case in criminal defense after that. I think she felt embarrassed for losing my case or something."

Astounded, McGinnis raised his eyebrows. "So you called her as soon as you were out?"

"Yes. At first, she acted as though she had never heard of me before, and she ignored me for almost five years. But then, maybe eight months ago or so, she suddenly contacted me."

"Wait, what? Leslie contacted you?"

"Yes. She had apparently looked for me all over the place. It was not necessary, as I was already living in the Pasadena area. She apologized for not having remembered me and offered to have my record sealed as her way of making amends. I was having a real hard time getting my life back. Nobody wants to hire somebody with a prison record, nor do they want to rent a room to you. So of course, I believed her and was immediately in on the deal. I did not know that there was a catch." She dropped her head back into her hands and shook her wet curls.

"You mean she asked you to do something in return for sealing your record?"

Marisella lifted her head up and looked McGinnis straight in the eye. "Yes. She's apparently an old friend of the police chief in Pasadena or something. At least, that's what I understand, because otherwise I don't get why she would have even bothered to connect me with him."

"Wait, what? Leslie Meyers was in on the deal?" McGinnis asked incredulously.

Marisella nodded. "The chief. Or Bartholdo, as you call him." She glanced at McGinnis. "He transferred ten grand into Leslie's account, which she then gave to me in cash. You were right, Mr. McGinnis. The printout that I put in your apartment was a hint. I'm really sorry I wrecked your apartment. But I had to make it look like a break-in, or else it would have been too obvious."

Lopez looked at McGinnis. "Boy, she broke into your apartment?"

McGinnis nodded. "Let me guess. You are also the one who planted my Beretta next to Alfio's body?"

Marisella looked down in shame. "Yes, I did."

"So *you* shot him?" Lopez had to ask.

McGinnis put a hand on Lopez's shoulder. "Wait, wait. Let her tell the whole story. Go on, Marisella."

Marisella nodded. "I stole your gun when you and the other guy came to my apartment the first time. I knew you had an ankle holster because I saw you adjust it from the window."

"I knew it!" McGinnis shouted.

Marisella grimaced.

"Go on, Miss Wawrinski," Lopez ordered. "So your old lawyer gave you money that the chief gave her? And then what?"

Marisella looked down. "She arranged a meeting. I was to get rid of Alfio and make it look like the detective did it. Then he would give me forty thousand more."

"Shutterbusters! Then it was all about the damn Tyrone Bastille case all along!" McGinnis almost shouted. "But why Helen? What did she have to do with all that?"

Marisella sighed deeply, and a deep crease formed between her eyebrows. "She found out! The bank statement that I planted in your apartment, she brought it home. She found a note with Alfio's and my name on it on Leslie's desk. The whole thing was planned. They knew Helen and Alfio were dating. That's why they gave me the money. So I could move in with her."

"The fact that Helen was expecting a baby with him didn't stop you?" McGinnis asked, astounded.

"I know!" Marisella sighed. "It is unforgiveable. I think the only way I was even able to do it was because I thought that she didn't care about him. But she did!"

"What do you mean? How did you figure out that Helen cared about Alfio?"

Marisella took a deep breath. "On the night that Helen...died, she confronted me. She showed me the bank statement and told me that she thought I was going to hurt Alfio. Apparently, she had been spying on me ever since she saw my name and Alfio's name on Leslie's desk. She heard my conversations with Bartholdo. She knew something was wrong."

McGinnis scratched his scalp. "Oh, okay. I am starting to get this. And because Bartholdo is the chief of the Pasadena Police, she was afraid to call the police?"

"Yes! She confronted me, and of course, that night Alfio had to walk in on us. We were in the midst of a fight. I was already half willing to let her talk me out of it. But then Alfio walked in. She was so furious. I knew she was going to tell him. I just could not face Helen telling Alfio that I was going to get rid of him, so I had to silence her. Alfio, of course, was devastated."

"Let me guess. There used to be a rug in your hallway?"

Marisella sighed. "We rolled her in the rug, and I made Alfio help me get rid of her. You might still find it in the dumpster at the horse stables."

"And Alfio just did what you said?" McGinnis asked in disbelief.

"He was cooperative because he did not want to get caught up in another crime while he was on probation. And I had the gun, of course. That helped. We went in his truck."

"The tracks!" McGinnis sighed out loud. "Oh, so when I came and interrogated you, that was the perfect opportunity for you to take my weapon so you could make it look like I did it."

Marisella nodded and looked down.

Lopez began to catch on. "But why didn't you shoot him with McGinnis's weapon?"

"I'm not used to it. If I was going to kill him, he was going to have to die immediately. I didn't trust myself to use the detective's weapon, because I was worried I would miss. I already screwed up with Helen. At least he wouldn't have to suffer."

"Oh my God!" McGinnis said, shaking his head. He glanced at Lopez. "Do you have all that?"

"Yup. Got it all in here." Lopez pointed at his iPhone, which was recording the entire conversation.

Then Marisella put her head in her hands again and began to sob. "I killed both! Helen was never supposed to die. But she knew! I had to do it. Aw! It hurts so bad. I killed my two best friends! I wish I could have just stayed in Linwood."

Lopez stood up, found a box of tissues, and brought it to her.

At that moment, somebody knocked on the door. McGinnis and Lopez exchanged a glance.

"That could be the suicide prevention professional. What was her name?"

Marisella looked up. "Audrey Simpson."

"Yeah, right."

"Suicide prevention? What the hell is going on today? You mean she tried to...? I don't understand anything." Lopez looked at McGinnis for help.

"Guess why we're all soaking wet. We had to get her off the Colorado Bridge. She was trying to jump."

"Oh my God. I think I'm going to get a drink."

The person knocked again.

"No. Go see who is knocking at that darn door so we can get some dry clothes on!"

Savalas was standing at the door with a pile of fresh, dry clothes. "I think you are going to wear a uniform today," Savalas said to McGinnis, extending the pile of clothes.

McGinnis picked up the uniform and grabbed a pair of jeans and a sweater for Marisella. He handed them to her and said, "Here. For you. Lopez will get somebody to show you where to change."

Lopez grabbed the phone again. "Officer Jackson. Yes, please."

A female officer appeared in the doorway. "That for her?" she asked Lopez.

"Yes. Show her where she can change."

"Yes, sir." To Marisella, she said, "Come with me."

Chapter Twenty-Two

After leaving Marisella in custody downtown, under the supervision of the currently sober Orlando Lopez and Audrey Simpson, McGinnis and Savalas were back in Savalas's green Honda, headed toward Pasadena. Both cops were unusually silent.

McGinnis unbuttoned the sleeves of his new shirt, which had started to cut off the circulation in his forearms. It was way too short for him. "Ah, much better," he said. He then proceeded to open the buttons around his neck. "I haven't worn one of these in ages."

Savalas said, "Any ideas on how to go about getting a testimony from Leslie Meyers now that we know our boss will do everything in his power to stop the truth from being revealed?"

"Yes," McGinnis said, rolling down the window. The car was getting stuffy from the heat that had returned almost instantly after the rain had stopped, though it was nearly seven PM. "First off, no reports. We leave that up to Lopez. He's a good man. He will do the right thing, even if it means that he will have to start drinking again."

Savalas glanced at McGinnis while passing under a footbridge over the 110 in the South Pasadena area. He seemed to decide not to say anything.

"Secondly," McGinnis went on, "we confront her directly. With zero warning. So she cannot tell Bartholdo. We let her know we have the evidence and offer her a plea deal."

Savalas stepped on the breaks to avoid hitting a car that was coming off of the too-short entry ramp. "Aw, they really ought to fix this freeway," he complained. "These ramps are impossible!"

"They're never gonna fix those. They'd have to rip down half of the city to build bigger ramps. Houses are way too valuable around here now."

"Yeah, I guess you got a point there. Anyway, what were you suggesting, exactly? That we head straight to her house? It's after seven, so chances are that we might catch her there. And if not, nobody knows that we were there."

"Except the entire neighborhood if we walk in dressed in police gear. Everybody knows everything in that little canyon. So, plan change. We stop at my apartment first and change into normal clothes. At least you are in your private car. That will give us some cover."

"You mean...I am going to wear your clothes?" Savalas asked. A rare frown became visible on his forehead.

"Exactly. Don't worry. We will find something for you. There was a time I was about your size, and I don't throw away clothes."

"Great." Savalas sighed. He had reached the end of the historic Arroyo Seco Parkway and stopped at the red light.

* * *

After grabbing some clothes at McGinnis's apartment, McGinnis and Savalas got in the car on Holliston Avenue and headed north on Sierra Madre Boulevard.

"You know where you're going?" McGinnis asked.

"No, not really. I was hoping you could give me the directions."

"No worries, pal. I got this. Just go straight until you hit town, and then head up on Baldwin. I'll show you the rest."

When they arrived in Little Santa Anita Canyon, Savalas and McGinnis left the car in the public lot next to Mary's Market and walked the rest of the way. By the time they reached Leslie Meyer's house, McGinnis was panting. Savalas already had his hand on the doorbell.

"Wait! Give me a minute. Let me catch my breath," McGinnis said.

Savalas withdrew his hand.

McGinnis exhaled and inhaled a couple of times. "Okay, I'm good."

"Sure you're all right?"

"Yes! Go ahead and ring the darn bell."

Savalas rang the bell. It took only about three seconds for Andrew Farzem to open the door.

"Oh, you again?" Farzem said. He appeared surprised to see them. "Anything I can help you with?"

"No. Actually, we were hoping to speak to your wife."

"Leslie? Sure. Let me go and get her. Why don't you come on in?"

As Farzem went to get his wife, McGinnis and Savalas entered an astonishingly chaotic entryway, with shoes, jackets, and bags strewn all over the floor. A glance into the living room proved that the organization in the other rooms was no better.

Farzem came back and said, "She will be here in a minute. Oh, and I apologize for the mess. Ever since Helen left us, we are back to our old chaotic habits. Why don't you have a seat?" He offered the two cops a seat on the couch. Piles of folders lay scattered over half of it. "Let me get those out of the way."

He was about to grab the pile when Leslie finally came down the stairs and said, "No! Those are mine. I'll take care of them."

Farzem dropped the folders back in their spot. "I guess you are going to have to use that half, then." He pointed toward the other part of the gray suede couch, which had seen better days.

Empty coffee cups and unwashed glasses rested on a glass coffee table that desperately needed to be wiped clean. McGinnis used his sleeve to sweep away a pile of breadcrumbs covering his place on the couch before sitting down.

"Glass of water?" Farzem offered.

"That's fine, thank you." McGinnis said.

"What about you?"

"No, thanks," Savalas replied.

Leslie, who was dressed in a matching dark- and light-blue sweatsuit extended her hand. "Leslie Meyers. How can I help you?"

"Pasadena PD. We have questions regarding our current homicide investigation. I am sure Mr. Farzem has told you about Helen Johnson's tragic ending," McGinnis said. It did not escape him how she was pretending she did not know him.

"Helen Johnson? Oh yes, it is very tragic. It's really too bad. She was so well... organized. Ever since she left... Look at this place! We are lost without her."

Farzem, who had gone into the kitchen, came back with a pitcher of water and glasses.

"That should be fine, Andy. I don't think they need you here, do you?" Leslie gave McGinnis and Savalas a questioning glance.

"I don't think so, no. We only need to speak with Mrs. Meyers right now," McGinnis said.

"Sure. I'll go disappear in my office, then," Farzem said, walking out.

"Concerning Miss Johnson, Dr. Farzem has told us that your opinion of her was not always as positive as you make it sound today," McGinnis began. He was curious about how she would respond to the gentle push.

Savalas raised his eyebrows in astonishment.

"Me? Wha-what? I don't know what you...what he means. She has been a fabulous help to our household!"

Leslie's denial fooled neither Savalas nor McGinnis.

McGinnis decided he would give her one more chance. "To be more specific, Mr. Farzem appeared to remember a change in your appreciation of Mrs. Johnson. He thought that you had changed your opinion of her during the course of your working relationship with her."

"Of course! She was flirting with my husband! How was I supposed to feel? It's not like she never... Rosie Gardener suspected an affair between Helen and her husband for years. She could just never prove it!"

"Ah, I understand," McGinnis said. He pulled out a copy of the bank statement that Marisella had planted in his apartment. "We actually think that your change in behavior has something to do with this here." He showed it to her. "Marisella, whom we know you are well acquainted with, has the original. I don't need to tell you whose name this statement is in. We believe that Helen Johnson was the first one to find it. And let me guess. She confronted you with it?"

Leslie looked at the printout and then at McGinnis. She laughed at him straight in the face. "What? Are you trying to scare me with some phony piece of paper? Seriously? You don't have any better tricks up your sleeve?"

"Let me tell you like it is, Mrs. Meyers. You can either remain in denial and defend yourself at court in a case of conspiracy to murder, or you can make your life easy and begin to cooperate. We know that the chief of the Pasadena PD paid you that money to put him in touch with Miss Wawrinski. We are also aware that you must have known something about his plans to get rid of Mr. Cordini, which he hired Marisella for. What we don't know is why a successful judge like you would stoop to such low levels to help a man who obviously has criminal intentions."

Leslie gasped. "How did you...? What are you...? This is outrageous!" She stood up and began pacing around the living room. She did not bother to look at her guests, who watched her every move. She suddenly stood still, took off her glasses, wiped them nervously on her sweat jacket, and put them back on. "You mean Marisella has the printout of the statement that Helen stole? How did she get her hands... Oh my God!" She sighed. "I think I need to sit down."

"Have some water," Savalas said. He poured water into a glass and handed it to her.

She took it and drank some. "She...she must have confronted her. Helen went to Marisella, and...and then Marisella... Oh my God...that's how it happened! What a stupid girl! I told her to stay out of it!"

"All right, Mrs. Meyers. We understand. What happened was very horrible. Nobody wanted that. However, what we don't understand is why would a woman like you would ever agree to help such a scoundrel like Bartholdo Meane."

Leslie took another sip of water, then looked from McGinnis to Savalas and back to McGinnis. "Leslie Meyers is not my real name. I changed my name many years ago. My real name is Leslie Meane," she said, setting her glass down.

"You are Bartholdo's sister?"

Leslie nodded. "Since we live in the same area, I changed my name so it would not be so obvious that we are connected. I defended him in one of his many cases of police brutality. This was one of the first cases of my career. He killed a black kid who had stolen a pack of cigarettes and was on the run. It was totally unjustified, but at the time it was an easy thing to get a white cop off the hook. For me, it was the perfect case to start out my career, so I agreed to do it. There were a couple more instances when I had to defend him. Every time I got him off the hook, he reminded me that it was thanks to him that I was so successful. I hated it. And I hated that I had won the cases. When I lost Marisella's case—a case which I finally felt very passionate about—I decided to change my career and went into family law." She picked up the water glass and took another sip.

McGinnis shrugged. "Possibly, you got a point there. Still, I don't get why you gave him Marisella's information," he said. "How did that even come to be?"

"It was at a party. Yes, I think at the Gardener's house. I was there, and Bartholdo was there. I must have briefly mentioned that Marisella had tried to contact me. He was immediately interested and pushed me to find her. When I had finally tracked her down in Pasadena, he told me he would pay me ten grand to organize a meeting. I said I didn't want the money, so he told me to give it to her as a down payment. I thought that was strange, but I didn't think much of it. I had no idea that he was planning to set you up...in such a despicable way."

"How did you find out?"

"Helen! Maybe you've heard from Andrew that she was not exactly as silent as a tree. She told us all about her new roommate. When I heard the name, I was stunned. It did not take me long to find out that Helen was dating your archnemesis. I put two and two together, so to say, but then Helen saw my bank papers. I did not know that she actually copied them. And she must have begun to ask questions.

"When Andrew came back on Sunday morning... Oh, horrible! Of course I did not want anything like that to happen to her. Even if I was jealous." She put her hands on her cheeks and shook her head. "Oh my, oh my, what have I done! Oh my, oh my!"

Savalas stopped the recording he was making on his phone. "Mrs. Meyers, we have recorded your testimony. Do you allow us to use it against your brother in the cases of Alfio Cordini and Helen Johnson?"

"Yes, I do."

"I think that should be enough to launch an official investigation at the Pasadena Police. What do you think?" McGinnis said.

Savalas nodded. "Marisella's testimony and Mrs. Meyer's appear to match. So I see no problem getting Bartholdo suspended."

"And hopefully away from the police for a long time," McGinnis said.

"That's the idea," Savalas said.

McGinnis turned back to Leslie. "All right. Another thing. I am going to forward your information to Tyrone Bastille's lawyer, who will also have great interest in your testimony since it might help in his case against Mr. Meane. May I forward your contact information?"

"Honestly, I have been looking for ways to correct my former missteps as a criminal defense lawyer. None of the kids that Bartholdo hurt should have experienced such abuse. When I heard about Helen, and then Alfio, it finally dawned on me what kind of a person Bartholdo really is. He will do anything to advance his agenda."

"Thank you for your willingness to serve justice, Mrs. Meyers. The lieutenant and I will arrange for a security team to protect you and your husband."

Farzem stepped out of his office and came back into the room. "Protect who?"

McGinnis and Savalas stood up, and McGinnis said, "Protect you and your wife. Mrs. Meyers has agreed to testify in two cases against our current police chief. Considering the extent he has gone to in order to silence my testimony, I would not put it past him to try the same thing with you and your wife. Your wife, mainly."

"Leslie is in danger?" Farzem put an arm around Leslie's waist.

"I'm going to be fine. They're sending a security team."

"Oh no! Then the whole neighborhood is going to know that you are testifying!"

McGinnis and Savalas exchanged a glance.

"Not if you don't tell them!" McGinnis said.

"You have no clue, Mr. Ginnis. The people in this canyon are terrible. They find out everything!"

"McGinnis," the detective said, lifting his hat. "Good night."

Chapter Twenty-Three

The following days were nothing short of madness. Savalas and McGinnis had to transfer their entire investigation to downtown LA, where they finalized their case. Neither Savalas nor McGinnis stepped foot in the Pasadena headquarters while their case was open. The official excuse was that they both had caught a cold during the rescue mission under the Colorado Bridge, which, in McGinnis's case, was not so far from the truth.

Savalas had requested that there be an investigation into the current and past actions of Bartholdo Meane. The investigation was granted without further delay, which meant that Bartholdo was temporarily removed from his position as the Pasadena PD chief. This was a good thing, for he had been driving the entire staff of the Pasadena PD mad by constantly requesting the location of a certain Marisella Wawrinski, who was obviously the person who had been rescued from the underside of the Colorado Bridge. Only, nobody from the Pasadena Police had a clue where she had gone. It was as if she had vanished, along with the two investigating officers, George Savalas and Peter McGinnis.

The subpoena for Leslie Meyer's bank account was no longer an issue, as she immediately allowed them to look into the payments from the chief. It was as if she had been waiting to finally be caught for her and her brother's inappropriate actions.

Bob Crany was in the best of spirits. With Michael James's recording, which had now been accepted as official evidence—to the utter dismay of the defense—Leslie Meyer's testimony, and the investigation into and temporary removal of the police chief, things were looking better than anticipated.

McGinnis only needed to tie together the loose ends of his case and back up some of the facts from Marisella's testimony. For instance, due to the secret nature of the investigation, Savalas himself—not some lower officer from the Pasadena PD—had the very pleasant task of verifying the location of the rug from Marisella's hallway. Savalas told McGinnis that there was no way that it would still be in the dumpster, especially considering that trash day in that area was on Mondays. McGinnis, however, insisted that Savalas go check anyway. And sure enough, after Fiona gave him the key and sent Max to help him shovel out the horse manure, the rug, which had gotten stuck to both sides of the dumpster, was still in there. Consequently, Savalas was forced to crawl in and manually pull it out.

The unraveled carpet, which was, of course, delivered to the forensics department that was investigating the case, not only confirmed that the fibers found at the crime scene matched the ones on the carpet, but it also confirmed that the blood stains on it matched Helen's DNA and the blood stains on Marisella Wawrinski's wall. Fibers from the same carpet were also found on Alfio Cordini's truck, which further corroborated the story that Marisella had told them. The tire prints, which forensics had secured at the original scene, were from the Toyota's front wheel.

Marisella had turned in the murder weapon, her Browning Buckmark, of her own free will, which McGinnis sent to his old friend Jack Pepperstone. Matching the two fired bullets to the weapon was now merely a formality.

A few more conversations with Marisella had revealed that she had been trained as a sharpshooter in the Navy Seal Corps, which explained how she was able to hit Helen right between the eyes.

The thing McGinnis looked forward to least was the testimony he was going to have to give in the actual Tyrone Bastille trial. Not because he was worried that Crany was going to lose—he was not—but because he knew he was going to have to face his former boss, who was going to attempt to pull

God knew how many more foul tricks in order to save his reputation and ruin McGinnis and Savalas in the process. However, McGinnis was not too worried. Given the current state of the evidence and testimonies, Barthold Meane's career was, to say it bluntly, over.

* * *

It was Friday evening by the time McGinnis and Savalas were able to pull together all the evidence and finally wrap up the case that had lain so heavily on McGinnis's soul. Savalas, who was giving McGinnis a ride from downtown, was just driving around the corner to Nell's house when McGinnis's phone rang.

"Oh, I think I know who that is!" McGinnis hit the green answer button. "Let me guess. My car is ready?" he spat into the cell phone. A smile played around on McGinnis's lips. "What? East Villa Street? Sure! We will be there in minutes." He hung up.

Savalas had just pulled over in front of Nell's Café.

"Make a right turn on Blanche Street. We are getting my car!"

Savalas snickered. "About time!"

* * *

Savalas let McGinnis out at 1435 East Villa Street, which was adjacent to Bungalow Heaven. He was parked on the curb in front of a ramshackle Craftsman construction. Ivy was growing all over the canopy and side walls of the wooden façade. The green paint was peeling off.

McGinnis stepped out of the Honda. "Get some rest over the weekend. I'm sure Bartholdo's lawyer has some unpleasant surprises ready for the trial."

"I expect nothing else," Savalas said.

Zeke rolled out the freshly painted nineteen-seventies Futura from behind his driveway. It was a perfectly polished shiny red. Both McGinnis and Savalas turned their heads.

"Red?" McGinnis said.

Savalas chuckled. "Nice!"

"You're kidding, right?" McGinnis asked self-consciously.

Savalas studied the car. "No, actually, I think it looks pretty good. He did a great job."

Zeke came over to the curb. "What do you say, boss? Neat, isn't it?"

"All right, I'm taking off," Savalas said.

McGinnis shut the passenger door, and Savalas drove off.

"It would have never occurred to me to paint the old tub red, but it looks good!"

"I added a new motor, new tires, and new breaks, and I updated all the electronics and changed all the fluids. It runs beautifully, purrs like a cat. Wanna test it?"

"What's the total?" McGinnis asked skeptically.

"For you? Four thousand. Believe me, it's a good price. I'm not even charging you for the spy work."

"We'll make it five, then," McGinnis said. He pulled his checkbook out of a pocket in his tweed blazer, which he had thrown over his shoulder. He wrote out the check and handed it to Zeke. "Here!"

"Oh man, thank you, boss!"

"Stop calling me that and give me the darn keys!" McGinnis said.

Zeke broke out into a huge grin that went from ear to ear. "Here, boss. Enjoy the ride!" He threw McGinnis the keys.

McGinnis opened the driver's side door. It did not make a sound. "Did you oil it?"

"That and some more," Zeke said proudly. "No more rust on your car. You're all set to sign up for your first classic car show!"

McGinnis climbed in. "Nice!"

The dashboard was all clean and shiny.

"You took good care of the inside of your car. I only had to change the front seats. Back is still original. Polished up the dashboard a little."

"Very nice!" McGinnis said, smiling for a change. He put on his seatbelt.

Zeke closed the door for him. "Have a nice ride, boss!"

McGinnis started the motor and took off.

* * *

McGinnis's suede beige slippers were placed meticulously at the edge of the bed. A duster with a pink, white, and red floral design was flung across the end of the bed. McGinnis was lying on his side of the bed, combing his chubby fingers through Nell's curly hair.

"So she spent twenty years in Linwood, and now she is going back for twenty more?" Nell asked incredulously. "What a waste of life!"

"Not if she helped take Bartholdo down. He apparently is responsible not only for covering up countless assaults on black people by the police but also for murdering one himself. At least, that's what his sister said."

"What about the murder of Alfio Cordini? Do you think they are going to make him responsible for that, or are they going to put all the blame on her, too?"

"The Helen Johnson murder clearly goes under her cap, although we are going to put in a plea deal due to the special circumstances. And I have no doubt Bartholdo is going to get sufficient time for his involvement in the murder of Alfio Cordini. Thanks to Marisella and Leslie Meyers, we have the entire money trail uncovered, so his intentions are easily proven."

"And what about Tyrone Bastille?"

At that moment, the telephone rang. "Aw, shutterbusters! At this time?" McGinnis grabbed his cell, accidentally ripping the charging cable out, and answered. "Detective!" he spat. "Yes, we're already in bed. What? He's going to testify? For real? That's amazing! Well, thank you very much for telling me. Yes. See you next week. Safe travels!"

McGinnis hung up and sat up in bed. "Oh, shutterbusters! Where is the darn power outlet?"

"It's behind the night table," Nell said.

McGinnis rolled out of bed, knelt on the floor with a loud *thump*, and searched the wall for the power outlet. He pushed the night table aside. "Ah, here it is!" He plugged in the cable and went back to bed. By the time he pulled the cover back over his body, he was huffing and puffing.

Nell could not suppress a smile. "What was that all about?" she asked.

"Oh, that was Crany. He somehow got the owner of the Seven Eleven shop to testify. Apparently, it was Bartholdo who had the video of Tyrone's assault removed."

"That's good news. How did he convince him?"

"Must've told him about Bartholdo's suspension. The negative publicity from some Black Lives Matters writers probably also helped."

McGinnis went back to combing through Nell's curls.

"I'm so glad things are starting to change for black folks," Nell said.

"Some folks never change. It's a shame. Just like in that Canyon of Shame. People pretend to be flawless when neighbors are looking, but when you look away, the truth about them comes out. Fred Wilson felt safe because he thought people wouldn't be looking when he kicked Tyrone in the back. But people are no longer ignoring police brutality. People are starting to see."

Nell, whose hair was starting to get all tangled, took McGinnis's hand and prompted him to stop. "Wait. What canyon are you talking about? I didn't get that."

"The Little Santa Anita Canyon."

"The one in Sierra Madre?"

"Yes, that one."

Nell's forehead wrinkled. She was deep in thought, so McGinnis sunk his hand back into her curls.

"Oh yes. Yeah, Little Santa Anita Canyon. The one where the houses are so close." Nell was silent for a moment, and her forehead continued to wrinkle. Then the crease between her brows left as her face lit with recognition.

McGinnis sighed. He carefully removed his hands from Nell's hair and kissed her on the forehead. Nell kissed him back on the lips.

"Shutterbusters, I'm tired." He turned around and shut off the light.

Acknowledgments

First and foremost, I want to thank all my friends and family members for your ongoing support. Thank you for believing in me.

Next, I would like to thank Professor Joseph Bentz from Azusa Pacific University who encouraged me to work on parts of my novel as my final thesis project. It is only thanks to your encouragement that I found the will and perseverance to finally get this thing done. Thank you, also, Dr. Windy Petrie for jumping on board with this project despite your family health issues, and for providing so many interesting and inspiring background works.

Thank you Kara Trummel, former neighbor, dog lover, and dear friend for proofreading my entire story and for helping getting it submission ready. Another shout-out goes to my dear friend Kim Clymer-Kelley Kissinger, cat lover, and Santa Anita Canyon resident. Thanks to your local knowledge you were able to save my story from a major error!

Thank you also Lorna Partington, writer and editor, UK, who was part of this story at its very early stages. You steered me away from some major technical gaffes.

Thank you, Chanie Garner from Jan-Carol Publishing, Inc., for doing the final edits on this project and for getting it print ready.

About the Author

Faye Duncan is a writer from the San Gabriel Valley, California. She is the author of *Murder on Wilson Street*, the first part of *The Bungalow Heaven Mystery Series*. She has published several short stories and volunteers as a script reader for International Film Festivals. Faye has an undying passion for ballroom dancing and lives with her son Max and her two dogs, Sammie and Lamby.

Fayeduncan.com
Facebook.com/fayeduncanauthor

CPSIA information can be obtained
at www.ICGtesting.com
Printed in the USA
JSHW060317280722
28637JS00003B/12